THE AMISH COWBOY'S WEDDING QUILT

AMISH COWBOYS OF MONTANA
BOOK X

ADINA SENFT

 Formatted with Vellum

"Any book that can both entertain and leave me thinking is a book worth reading! Adina Senft is quickly becoming one of my favorite writers of Amish fiction.... Senft's characters are beautifully developed, [and] will move you to both laugh and cry."

— CHRISTIAN FICTION ADDICTION

CAST OF CHARACTERS
THE AMISH COWBOY'S WEDDING QUILT

CAST OF CHARACTERS

The Millers at the Wild Rose Amish Inn

- Rachel Zook Miller and Luke Hertzler (engaged to be married October 4)
- Tobias Miller, widower, father of twins Gracie and Benny, and Sylvia Keim (engaged to be married August 30)
- Gideon Miller
- Susanna Miller and Stephen Kurtz (engaged to be married October 11)
- Seth Miller

The Millers on the Circle M Ranch

- Reuben and Naomi Glick Miller
- Daniel and Lovina Wengerd Lapp Miller, Joel

- Adam Miller and Kate Weaver (engaged to be married November 10)
- Zach Miller and Ruby Wengerd (engaged to be married at spring breakup next year)
- Malena Miller and Alden Stolzfus (engaged to be married January 12)
- Noah and Rebecca Miller King
- Joshua and Sara Fischer Miller, Nathan
- Deborah Miller (age 1)

The King family

- Arlon and Kate King
- Annie Gingerich (91, Kate's aunt)
- Simeon (engaged to Susan Bontrager)
- Noah (married to Rebecca Miller)
- Clara
- Patricia

THE AMISH COWBOY'S WEDDING QUILT

THE CIRCLE M RANCH

Friday, August 5 at 11:30 a.m.

GIDEON MILLER HAULED on the wrench one last time. "Okay," he called to his younger brother Seth. "Let it flow." They were knee-deep in the irrigation ditches on the Circle M, and if this little bit of persuasion didn't work on the water gate, they were going to have to get serious with the shovels.

Seth leaned on the lever that changed the direction of the water flow in this section, and it barely squealed as it opened and the water poured into the channel. Before it reached him, Gideon leaned on the gate that hadn't been opening properly, and it gave obediently under his hands. Gideon's own relief was just about equal to the welcome gush of water that flowed over his bare feet and out into the thirsty grazing field.

He'd worked on the water gates before, but this one had been a bear. They couldn't very well leave the job to Reuben or one of their cousins, though. He and Seth might be family, but they were also paid hands, and the hands' job was to keep the irrigation system clean and the water flowing. The ranch's income depended on healthy fields and meadows, not only for the cattle in the home pastures, but for the ones who would be coming down from the range allotments during roundup next month. Until the cattle trucks came to take them to market, the animals had to fatten up on healthy grass and increase their weight to bring the most value.

That money would keep the ranch going through the winter ... and maybe even allow Adam Miller to finish his house before the snow flew. He and Kate Weaver planned to marry in November, and the dream that drove her to cleaning houses as a *Maud* and him to long hours with hammer and saw was to have a finished house ready for the first day of their life together.

After Gideon rolled up his tools, then pulled on his socks and laced his boots, his stomach growled, telling him that it was nearly time for *Middagessen*, the midday meal up at the big house.

And kept growling.

Then he realized it wasn't his stomach at all—it was the sound of a big diesel pickup rumbling down the county highway.

"Right on time," he said to Seth, pushing up his straw hat with a forefinger to watch the red monster pass. He couldn't see which of the Madison boys from the Rocking Diamond dude ranch was at the wheel, but it didn't matter.

What mattered was the passenger he glimpsed through the truck's side window. A passenger wearing the bucket-shaped white *Kapp* of the Siksika Valley Amish women. A passenger who had no business riding in a worldly man's truck. Especially one of *those* worldly men.

"It's not your business, *Bruder*," Seth told him. "Your business and mine right now is lunch." Seth had his priorities.

But Gideon couldn't let it go. "Patricia King has brothers and a father. Why don't they say anything to her?"

"Maybe they don't know." Seth gathered up his own roll of tools and together they walked through the springy meadow grass to the ranch house about a quarter mile away. "Or maybe it just makes sense that after she gets done with her job on the dude ranch, one of them takes her into town to the quilt shop for her second job. Not everyone gets to lollygag in meadows like us."

There was nothing more aggravating than when the youngest of the Miller siblings made sense. But sometimes sense meant more than the logistics of getting from one job to the next every day. "She's spending too much time around worldly people."

"You forget how lucky as we are," Seth pointed out. "We have family who just happened to need what we had to offer when we moved here."

"Noah and Simeon should find a way to give her a job. They do construction. Someone has to send bills and stuff. It should be her."

"Rebecca might disagree with you. She's pretty happy about running the office side of King Construction. She'll be even happier when she can do it from her own home instead of here."

Rebecca had been born and raised on the Circle M, but even with its welcoming size and seemingly infinite capacity to add just one more, newlyweds needed their own home. Her husband Noah King and his brother Simeon were building theirs even now, on a little oddly shaped parcel Mamm had deeded to them between the Wild Rose Amish Inn's land and that of the Zook brothers. Noah loved Rebecca so much that, even as Jacob in the Bible had worked and waited for his Rachel, he was willing to work and wait for their own home.

"Still. Someone should be looking after his sister before she gets herself into *Druwwel*."

"What trouble can she get into on a ten-minute drive?"

"It's the Madisons," he said grimly. "Anything is possible."

"I think you need some food to change your outlook." They opened the pasture gate and walked up the short, hard-packed cattle lane to the back of the barn. The bunkhouse formed the top floor of the barn, built above the buggy area, the horse stalls, and the cattle pens, and slept six hands. They were the only ones living there at the moment.

They washed up and joined the family for lunch in the big house, which sat on a rise of ground a little higher than the barn and outbuildings. His Aendi Naomi's skill in the kitchen was another reason Gideon was grateful to have work on the Circle M. He was secretly looking forward to roundup, not because of the excitement of driving the cattle down the mountain, but because her famous elk stew at the end of the last day was said to be what brought more of the neighbors to help than anything else.

But today's lunch was pretty *gut*, too. After a silent grace, he and Seth dug in to barbecued sausage, corn on the cob, onion rings in a tasty batter, and a salad that seemed to burst with every vegetable growing in Naomi, Rebecca, and Malena's garden out back.

"Did you get that gate closest to the highway working again?" Onkel Reuben asked.

"*Ja*, we did," Gideon told him. "The flanges were seized up, like you thought."

Reuben, who was a man of few words, nodded in satisfaction.

"We'll be checking the others this afternoon," Seth put in. "If one was seized, others might be thinking about it. Better to catch them now than in the middle of a blizzard."

"I don't know," Kate Weaver said thoughtfully. "Your sister Susanna caught Stephen Kurtz in the middle of a blizzard with no trouble at all."

Everyone around the huge ranch table roared with laughter. Even Gideon had to admit that as zingers went, it was a pretty good one,. Adam grinned at his smarty-pants fiancée, then turned back to Gideon. "Want me to give you a hand out there?"

Seth was already shaking his head. "*Ischt gut, denki.* You need to be working on that house of yours. Two more months and we just might get a blizzard. I hear that around the Siksika, snow can surprise you in September as well as May."

They had only moved here in February, but after the freak blizzard that had trapped their sister overnight with her ex, along with Zefra Harris, the young woman who was the house manager at the Rocking Diamond, and her little son, Gideon was willing to believe anything of the Montana weather.

And thinking of the Rocking Diamond brought him right back around to Patricia King.

"One of the Madison boys took Patricia in to work just now," he said. "Maybe Rebecca ought to talk to Noah about it."

Aendi Naomi looked a little startled. "About what? The girl has to get from one job to another somehow on the days she works late."

"She could drive a buggy, like everyone else."

"They collect her in the morning, Gideon," Aendi Naomi said as if he didn't know, as if that didn't make the situation worse. "She doesn't have a buggy. It's kind of them to put themselves out on the days Zefra doesn't go and get her."

"The Rocking Diamond isn't that far from the King place," he said defensively. "She could walk it easily."

"In the summer," his cousin Malena pointed out. "Nobody's walking that in the winter unless they're desperate."

"Besides," her brother Zach said quietly, "what Patricia King does is no business of ours."

"I already told him that," Seth, the traitor, said around his sausage.

Gideon looked up to argue, but caught Onkel Reuben's eye. His uncle swallowed a bite and said to no one in particular, "Seems like a lot of interest in that girl for her being nobody's business."

Which embarrassed Gideon so much that he was silent as a stone all the way through the meal and the apple pie and ice cream that followed.

When he and Seth returned to the irrigation project that afternoon, he made sure to put two or three of the home fields between himself and his brother. The last thing he needed was another dose of teasing. Because what was Patricia King to him? Their cousin Rebecca's sister-in-law, that was all. A girl he saw at church every other Sunday, at singing, at the volleyball games on Friday nights. Once in a while here at the Circle M, when his aunt and uncle invited Noah's family on off Sundays for informal fellowship and lots of good food.

A girl who probably didn't realize he was even a face in the crowd. Who people wanted to be around not only because her off-kilter view of the world made them laugh, but because her own laugh was enough to make you smile just hearing it from across the room. Her looks were the second thing you noticed about her—the nut-brown hair always trying to escape from under her covering, the clear eyes that were green in the sunlight and grey on a cloudy day. And the matched set of dimples ... well, there were plenty of young men who cracked jokes around her just to see them dent her cheeks.

Not he. Gideon had a healthy enough sense of humor, but he was not about to make a spectacle of himself just to get a girl to smile.

If she wanted to make a spectacle of herself riding around in showy trucks with her employer's sons, that was up to her.

And if he attacked the next stiff gate with more enthusiasm than it deserved, well, it was because he was conscientious about his uncle's business, that was all.

❦

PATRICIA KING HAD LEARNED SHE HAD TO GET OUT OF Chance Madison's truck in two stages. First you had to slide off the seat to the running board while hanging on to the door, and then you could jump down from the running board to the concrete. But it was easier to talk from the running board; you didn't feel like a *kleiner Kind* stretching up to see the driver.

"Thanks, Chance. I appreciate the ride."

"Anytime," he said easily. "I was going in to the library anyhow."

She squinted at him. She'd only been working at the Rocking Diamond a month, but even in that short length of time she'd never seen any evidence he knew books existed. "You are not."

He held up his hands in innocence. "Truth. Zefra asked me to borrow the next book in that series Matty likes. He finished the one about the dog, and now he's on to crazy animals that rescue things."

"He's done with Carl?"

"The books don't have any words, so it beats me why anybody would look at them, but Zefra says she's read them all to him."

"That's Carl."

"Anyway, I'll have to ask at the library about these rescue books. Kids' books all look the same to me."

Considering she and her sister Clara had loved Carl and his adventures so much the books had practically fallen apart, and the John Himmelman books were adorable, this was a head-shaker. *Head-shaker*. That was one of Brock Madison's expressions. Chance's father didn't really speak to her as she made beds and dusted in the guest wing, but she heard him often enough on the phone, talking to his business associates. She supposed every call made him more money, but that wasn't any of her business. Looking after the Rocking Diamond's guests was.

"The next one is *Duck to the Rescue*," she told him, hopping down to the pavement. "See you tomorrow."

She slammed the door, the diesel engine growled, and he backed out of the parking spot. A sedan full of tourists came to a screeching halt inches from his bumper and he didn't even seem to notice, just wheeled off down the highway in the direction of the library.

But that was Chance. He was a middle child, living in an uncertain world between his mean older brother Trey and his copycat younger brother Clint. But somehow he managed to navigate through it without losing arms or bumpers or even his temper.

She'd eaten an early lunch with her boss, Zefra, who was Taylor Madison's domestic assistant and thus responsible for everything that went on inside the walls of the big house and the guest houses. Patricia started at noon here at Rose Garden Quilts. Rose Stolzfus went home at five so that Patricia could have her dinner hour at four, and then Patricia worked until eight three days a week. The only thing she didn't like about working late on Friday nights was that if there were doings among the *Youngie*, not only did she have to find a ride over to wherever it was, she always arrived late and missed out on half the fun.

None of the Amish shops and businesses stayed open past four on Saturdays. Maybe that was inconvenient for the tourists, but Saturday evening was for preparing food ahead for Sunday, the family reading of the Bible, and for quiet time to prepare the heart for church the next day. At least, that was what their parents expected. But often in their shared room, Clara and Patricia didn't prepare much more than what dress they'd wear and speculate on whether any of the young men from the west district would visit for church.

"Hi, Patricia," Rose said with a smile, looking up from the broad wooden table where she was measuring yardage for a customer. A stack of bolts from a beautiful set of Robin Pickens fabrics waited on the side. "Want to take over here?"

Translation: *I'm starving and I'll faint before I get through all six of these bolts. Save me.*

"I'll just put my backpack away." She smiled at the customer and returned in half a minute, smoothly taking up the cutting shears.

"A yard of each, and four yards of that fifty-inch backing that goes with it," Rose said.

"This will be so beautiful," Patricia told the customer as Rose slipped out the door for the five-minute walk home. "Every time a set of her fabrics comes in, I want to make something out of it right away."

"I was like that with these," the customer, a woman in her thirties, said. "And you even have her patterns here. I couldn't resist." She tried not to look as though she was examining Patricia's dress, cape, and apron. "I thought Amish folks didn't use patterned fabric?"

"We do if we're making something for sale." With her chin, she indicated what Rose called the *fishing lure* hanging in the big front window. "Like that one."

She folded one bolt and picked up the next.

"That is one beautiful quilt. Did someone from here make it?"

Patricia felt her cheeks warm. "Yes—I did. But I don't mean to point it out because of that. I was just using it as an example. The fabrics we use in our quilts at home and for our clothes are over there." She tilted her head to the left. "Those colors are solids, all approved by the *Ord*—the church."

"And you have to wear only what's approved by the church?"

Patricia smiled as she moved on to the next bolt. "Some of us push the limits a little. This dress I'm wearing isn't *exactly* the approved shade of green that my mother would wear, for instance."

The customer chuckled. "It's pretty, though. It brings out the green in your eyes."

Zefra had told her that, too. The testimony of two men— or women, in this case—must be true.

She finished up the cutting, added pattern and thread, and rang up the sale.

"You take credit cards?" the woman asked in surprise. "Some Amish communities I've been to don't."

"It depends on the business," Patricia allowed. "Most of our customers are from away, so we have to be prepared. The wi-fi is shared by everyone on this side of the block, and we use this little tap thing. There you go."

The customer left with her big shopping bag full to the brim and a happy spring in her step, while Patricia had the satisfaction of seeing triple digits go through on the tap thing.

When Rose came back from lunch, they had a steady stream of customers. Patricia didn't even get a chance to put away the Pickens bolts before someone else wanted them cut, and a woman from Texas bought a set of the placemats Clara had made. Since the ready-made things were sold on consignment, she'd be pleased at the sixty percent.

Patricia ate her dinner in the break room in the back, then urged Rose to leave early. For once again it was a Friday night, and she'd already seen her son, Alden Stolzfus, close up his smithy and head home.

"Are there doings tonight?" Rose asked as she collected her handbag.

"A taffy pull over at Petersheims'," Patricia said. "It's just as well I have to work. Calvin Yoder is trying to get Cathy Petersheim's attention and you know as well as I do what's going to happen."

Rose pretended to shudder. "His hand is still in a cast. He can't pull taffy."

"He'll get himself wound into it like a great big lollipop, I guarantee it. With any luck, Cathy will wrap him in plastic and stand him in a corner to cure."

Her boss laughed at the image and headed out the door, leaving Patricia in charge for the next three hours.

If the stream of customers dried up, maybe she'd give herself an early night.

❀   2   ❀

MOUNTAIN HOME

AT SEVEN FORTY-FIVE the bell over the door jingled, and to Patricia's astonishment, Chance Madison walked in. He put his hands on his hips and surveyed the shop with its colorful bolts of fabric, the quilts hanging on the walls, and Patricia's quilt in the window.

"Nice place."

"Have you never been in here?" she inquired.

"Nope. Thought you might want a ride home."

That took her aback. Giving her a ride to town when he was going there anyway was one thing, but giving her a ride home was different. It was what an Amish boy did when he wanted to court you. But of course, an *Englisch* man wouldn't know that. Or want to do any such thing.

"I'm not going home," she said at last. "I was going to walk over to my boss's to see if anyone from her house is going late."

"To what?" He leaned a hip on the counter where the cash register stood.

She folded the fabric on the last of the bolts on a neat diagonal, tucked in the tail, and carried them over to return them to the stacks. "Just a volleyball game and a taffy pull."

"At the rec center? I know they have open volleyball nights over there, but I've never heard of them making candy."

"No, it's at an Amish place. Do you know the Petersheims? Out on Elk Flat Road?"

He shook his head. "You can give me directions. Ready?"

"Wait—what?" She paused in the act of pulling out the cash drawer.

"I can give you a ride over there. No big deal."

This was about seven different kinds of wrong. "Chance, I can't ask you to do that."

"You didn't. I offered."

"That's not the point." She shook her head. "I'll walk over to Rose's. Thanks for the offer, though."

"And what if no one's home?"

"Rose will be home." Maybe. If she wasn't over at the Zook brothers' for supper, or invited for coffee at the Wild Rose Amish Inn, or any number of places a bride-to-be in her forties might go on a Friday night. "Good night, Chance. I have to cash out, lock up, and make the bank deposit. The game and the taffy will probably be over by the time I get there anyhow."

He nodded, tapped the counter lightly with one hand, and ambled out. The bell jingled behind him and she let out her breath.

Imagine if she'd let him. She shook her head and started counting bills. Imagine rolling up to the Petersheim farm in front of every young person in the valley, in a big truck whose color Chance's father called *write-me-up red*. She would never, ever hear the end of it. No, scratch that. She would have made him drop her off half a mile away and pretended she'd walked the whole four miles from town.

With the fat deposit envelope and slip written up and in her backpack, she turned out the lights and locked up carefully. The bank was at the end of the next block, and was well lit. She'd never felt anything but safe in the Siksika Valley since they'd moved to Aendi Annie's old hay farm and brought it back to life. Annie Gingerich might be in her nineties, but she was one of Patricia's favorite people. There had been many an evening filled with chocolate chip cookies and laughter as she and Clara listened to her stories of the old days, when the first Amish families had come to the valley in the sixties and seventies. After the blizzard last May, the two of them had concluded that no matter how outlandish her stories sounded, even the one about climbing out on the roof to get out of the house after a blizzard was probably true.

Patricia made the deposit, the *clunk* of the tilt-out tray as it swallowed the envelope kind of satisfying. It meant the end of a good week. It meant food on the table and wages in her pocket on the fifteenth.

She had just crossed the parking lot, heading for the bridge and Rose's rented house beyond it, when a pair of headlights came on and lit her up like the ball field at the *Englisch* high school. She gasped and threw up one arm.

The lights went out immediately. "Sorry," came Chance Madison's contrite voice from inside the vehicle she hadn't even noticed, though you'd think that would be impossible. By night all cars were grey, evidently. "I forgot I had the high beams on. Sure you don't want that ride?"

On impulse, she put on her best schoolteacher voice. "I guess I'll have to. I'm blinded by your headlights and can't see a thing." He opened the passenger door for her from the inside and she reversed her process to climb in. "What were you thinking? You scared me."

"Sorry," he said again, pulling out without even looking. "There was a fifty percent chance that this was the right bank, so I was waiting for you."

"Take Creekside Drive all the way to the end and turn right. Can you really have nothing else to do on a Friday night but be an Amish taxi? What do you charge?"

"Nothing." He must be a very literal person, like her sister. "I just didn't like the thought of you walking at night. Some of these roads don't have streetlights."

"I know all the Amish people in town. Someone would have given me a lift. You really didn't have to do this, Chance."

"It's something different," he said with a shrug.

It certainly was. So was arriving at their destination five minutes after leaving the bank. In a buggy, the trip took half an hour—more if the weather was bad. But tonight was a warm August night, and here was the Petersheim mailbox already, popping out of the dark like a surprise.

"Wait—just drop me here, okay?"

"That's a long lane. Are you sure there's a house down there?"

"Yes, of course. But I don't want to—" She stopped.

"What?"

She chose her words carefully so as not to offend him. "It's just that it'll be all Amish folks there. I don't want to—" *Make a big show and cause a firestorm of gossip.* "—give people the wrong impression."

"Of what? Your boss's son trying to help?"

This was the trouble with being friends with the *Englisch*. The things that Amish people learned practically before they could walk and talk were impenetrable puzzles to outsiders.

"It's not that. I really appreciate your help. But all my friends, well..."

"Oh. I see. I'm not your friend. Or good enough for your church friends."

Oh help, she'd hurt his feelings. He had leaned a little away from her and was gazing out the windshield with his chin drawn in, like a turtle.

"Of course you are." And then another impulse prompted her to say, "All right. Park the truck by that cattle gate, off the road, and walk up with me. If you're any kind of volleyball player, they'll welcome you with open arms. Even if you're a bad one, they will. None of us play to win. It's just for fun."

"Yeah?" She couldn't see his eyes in the dark, but hope warmed his voice. "You sure they won't mind?"

"If they do, the first time you spike the ball and make a point, they'll change their minds. Come on."

GIDEON SWUNG HIS PALM AT THE VOLLEYBALL. HIS SIDE WAS up by six points, as near as anyone could figure, and it was his turn to serve. Just before he hit the ball, he happened to glance over it to see Patricia King walk up to the makeshift court with Chance Madison at her side.

He was so shocked that his hand went right past the ball and he dropped it. All five players on his side groaned as it rolled out of bounds and they lost the serve.

To add insult to injury, when they were up again, Patricia waved Chance into the game, and waited on the sideline to come in next.

The *Englisch* boy nodded at him. "Gid."

He hated people abbreviating his name. "Chance. This is a surprise."

"To me, too." The *Englisch* man served the ball with perfect form, sending it sailing over the net just low enough for the front row to miss it and have to return it. Several serves later, Chance asked him, "What's the score?"

"I don't know. A bunch."

"Game point," Chance called, and sent it over. After a fierce volley the other side missed, and the game was over. Not that anyone cared who won, but because Chance had clinched it, this just irritated Gideon more.

Everyone scattered to see what was going on with the taffy, so Gideon made his way over to Patricia. "You never got to play."

She shrugged. "I wasn't expecting to. But at least I might get some candy."

Chance walked up, and the next thing Gideon knew, Patricia was showing him how to butter his hands and they were pulling on a loaf-sized glob of white taffy with sprinkles like confetti in it.

"Come on, Gideon," Cathy Petersheim said, holding up a stick of butter. "It's boys and girls. Be my partner?" If ever a face communicated *pleeeease*, it was Cathy's.

He didn't want to know where Calvin Yoder was, but if there was a mess to be made, he'd be in the middle of it. Only a matter of time. Gideon's protective side made him smile and reach for the butter, briskly coating his hands. She scooped up a blue blob of warm taffy, and the two of them started pulling.

"Smells like bubblegum," he said, to make conversation after she'd instructed him how to pull properly.

"It is. The confetti is vanilla, and my sister should be bringing out the strawberry any minute. How was the game?"

"*Gut,*" he said. "Why are you speaking English?"

"Because we appear to have *Englisch* company and it's only polite."

Nobody invited him, he wanted to say. Except Patricia obviously had.

And then he had to quit being such a crank, because Cathy meant serious business with this taffy, and ten minutes later his forearms were beginning to ache. He nearly thanked *Himmel* when she finally said, "That's got it! Now, you roll it into a rope and I'll cut it into candy-sized pieces. Then we'll both wrap them with this waxed paper here."

He'd never rolled taffy in his life, but Cathy was a good teacher. And call him catty, but when their bowl of neatly wrapped taffy went into the line-up on the table for people to take some of each flavor home, he saw that Patricia and Chance were still struggling with the final stages of pulling. Granted, the candy was stiff and hard to handle when it got to that stage, and if it was the first time for both of them—

"Whoops!" The vanilla confetti taffy did a double flip and landed splat in the grass.

"Ach, neh!" Red-faced in the golden light of the lanterns strung around the tables, Patricia looked as though she might burst into tears.

Chance scooped it up and tried to brush off bits of grass and dirt, wood and who knew what else. "It kind of looks like green sprinkles," he said gamely.

"Absolutely not," Patricia said. "Chickens and goats have been walking around out here. Put it in the garbage."

"But we worked so hard on it. My arms are sore."

Patricia gently extracted the bristly glob from his buttery hands. "It's all right, Chance. It happens. Just be glad you're not—"

There was a crash and a scream from inside the house, and a second later the screen door slammed back as Calvin Yoder burst out of it, a mophead close behind him wielded with considerable energy by Sarah Jane Petersheim. "You stay out of this house, Calvin Yoder!" she shouted. "That's my whole batch of strawberry taffy you just ruined—you belong in the barn with the goats!"

His head tucked down like that mop was really going to land upside his head, Calvin loped away in the direction of the barn. Sticky pink footprints followed him across the grass.

"See?" Gideon heard Patricia say to Chance. "It could be worse—you could have upended a whole pot of boiling taffy instead of one little loaf."

"Is that girl okay?" he asked as the door slammed behind Sarah Jane. "Did she get burned?"

"I don't think so. But she needs some help cleaning up. You put this taffy in the trash while I give her a hand."

She gave it back to him and she and Cathy and a couple of the other girls hurried up the steps to help poor Sarah Jane clean up the pink flood no doubt already congealing on the kitchen linoleum.

Chance did as he was told, then ambled over to Gideon, who was wiping butter off his hands with a paper towel. He didn't really want to get into a conversation, but he and Seth were probably the only people here that Chance knew.

"Is it always this exciting in Amishlandia on Friday nights?"

What on earth was Amishlandia? "Not usually. Come on. There'll be a sink around back."

Seth joined them as they cleaned the last of the butter off their hands with hot water and soap. "Ever made taffy before, Chance?" his brother asked.

"Nope. Probably never will, either, unless they're doing this again next week."

"Not that I know of," Gideon said hastily. Best he didn't

get any ideas about making the *Youngie* part of his crazy social life. "How did you happen to arrive with Patricia?"

"I hung around to give her a ride home, but she was coming here, so I gave her a ride here instead." He made this unique behavior sound perfectly rational and normal.

"But ... why give an Amish girl a ride anywhere?" he persisted.

Chance shrugged. "She works for us. I take her into town all the time."

Gideon raised his eyebrows at his brother. *A little help here?*

"Right," Seth said, "but taking a girl home is a different thing."

"I don't see how. It's five miles no matter how you slice it."

"Well, among the Amish, it's more than that," Seth said. "If a girl lets a man take her home, it means she's open to his courting her."

Chance stared at him. "Courting. You mean, like, dating?"

Seth nodded.

Chance took a breath as though he'd just had a revelation. "That's why she wouldn't let me. Wow. I better talk to her."

"I think she probably gets that you didn't know," Gideon said. With any luck, that would be the end of it.

"But when I take her home tonight, I'll tell her it doesn't mean anything. It's just a ride."

Now Seth was looking as alarmed as Gideon felt. "I don't think you'd better do that, Chance."

"But if I just tell her—"

Gideon jumped in. "The thing is, her sister is here with the buggy. Patricia will probably go home with her. You don't need to go out of your way."

"It isn't out of my way. Nothing in this little valley is out of my way. And you know what the song says—you go home with him what brung you."

It took a lot to hang onto his patience, but Gideon did it. *Der Herr* must be watching out for him. "Patricia is Amish. It won't do her reputation any good to have everyone at church know she went home with someone who isn't. Think about her, Chance. What's good for her might be different from what you think is right."

He sounded like his own father, though the love and humor was missing from his voice. He'd give a lot for Dat to be alive right this minute, to walk over and give him a hand with this. Or even Dat's brother, Onkel Reuben. Reuben and Naomi had been managing Madisons for a decade now, and while the two families had their differences, they'd still remained good neighbors who—for the most part—understood and respected each other.

And then, as though *Gott* himself had heard his unspoken wish, Paul Petersheim joined them to wash his own hands, though he hadn't been pulling taffy with the *Youngie*. As the local butcher and meat processor for the hunters, he had forearms like hams—he wouldn't be feeling any soreness no matter how much taffy he pulled, for sure and certain.

"About time you headed home, *ja*?" Cathy and Sarah Jane's father said to Chance. "Been quite a night."

"Are they done in the kitchen?" Chance asked. "If Patricia—"

"She's not done," Petersheim said firmly. "It's going to take awhile and might just involve show shovels. Best you head on out and we'll look after Patricia. My regards to your parents."

And somehow, with Petersheim's hand on his shoulder and a bit of friendly conversation later, Chance walked off down the lane by himself, leaving Patricia safely among her own people.

"Remind me to thank him on Sunday," Gideon said in a low voice to his brother.

"What got into her, inviting an *Englisch* man to our doings?" Seth asked in a low voice. "And a Madison to boot. You might as well invite a coyote or a wolverine."

"Trey is the coyote, and Clint is a dog pretending to be one. I don't think Chance is that bad. Maybe he's a billy goat. Or one of those wild mustangs. Something that you think you can domesticate, but you really can't. Not without a lot of pain— on your part, not his."

"Let's hope Patricia sees that, too, and doesn't encourage him," Seth said. "Can't you talk to her?"

Gideon shook his head. "Not my place. But with any luck, Paul will have a word with Arlon King and that will be the end of it."

Seth didn't look convinced.

"Well, for pity's sake," Patricia said in exasperation as Clara shook the reins over their horse's back and they rolled briskly down the Petersheim lane. "Are you telling me those Miller boys just stood there while Paul Petersheim practically booted Chance off the property?"

"I wouldn't say *booted*." Clara was nothing if not precise, in everything from measuring flour to cutting fabric to choosing words. "He just told him it was time to go home, and that you'd be going home with me. He can tell anyone he wants to leave his property." She considered for a moment. "Except maybe the bishop. I don't think he'd do that."

"But—"

"Patricia, take a deep breath and think. What would Mamm and Dat say if Chance Madison and his big truck rolled into the yard with you?"

"They'd say thank you for bringing me home," Patricia said crossly. "And so would I."

"Maybe. But you'd get the lecture of your life once he was gone. And probably all my chores for the next week. While I'd love that, it's not worth it when we always go home together."

It made Patricia even more cross that her sister was right.

"Honestly, *mei Schweschder*, what were you thinking, inviting him tonight? He doesn't belong with us, and for sure you don't belong anywhere near him. Everyone in the valley knows the reputation of the Madison boys."

Sometimes her sister's blunt habits of speech went sailing right past honesty and into the danger zone of offense. "Chance isn't going to do anything. He gives me a ride whenever we're going the same way. That's all. What do you think I'm going to do, kiss him?"

Clara lost her grip on the reins for just a second. *"Neh!"*

They turned onto the county highway and picked up speed, the comforting sound of the horse's hooves on the pavement like the heartbeat of her life. Sometimes fast, sometimes slow, but always with a purpose. Always the same.

Maybe that was the trouble. Maybe this irritation tonight was all part of her dissatisfaction lately. This feeling that if she could just get away from the sameness of it all and do something exciting for once, she'd come back to regular life and be happy. Though what that exciting thing might be, she didn't know. People who went looking for excitement didn't tend to be Amish. That was for *Englisch* people.

Like the Madisons.

"Would you really kiss a worldly boy?" In the dark in the buggy, she didn't need to see Clara's face. Her tone expressed her distaste well enough.

"Good grief, I don't know. Leave it be, Clara. The whole church will be talking about this soon enough. I need some peace and quiet before it starts."

Clara had sense enough not to say, *Then you shouldn't have done something to make them talk.*

Some things were so obvious they didn't need to be said.

Sunday, August 7

PATRICIA AND CLARA, as the youngest of five, were only a year apart, with Clara the older. That meant they sat together in church toward the back of the women's side, among the single women seated in order of age. This also meant, sadly, that any young man you were interested in tended to be seated on the men's side even farther back. If you wanted to make eye contact, you had to turn around to do it, and no one in her right mind would do that in front of the whole *Gmay*. A fleeting glance by accident might not be detected, but a deliberate attempt? That would bring the wrath of Mamm down on you like a hen on a grasshopper. Or worse, the kind advice of the young marrieds in the family. As much as Patricia liked her sister-in-law Rebecca, she wasn't about to invite *that*.

Besides, there wasn't anyone back there who interested her. Irritated her, maybe. Rachel Miller's boys fell into that category. The Yoders, definitely. Calvin got a flat no, and she'd made good and sure David Yoder crossed her off his list, too.

When their family had first moved to the valley and she'd got wind of his tendency to pursue anything in a *Kapp*, she'd accepted one date with him. She'd deliberately shocked him by suggesting they go swimming at the rec center and he'd never asked for another.

She and Clara had hooted over that—until he'd asked Clara out. Big mistake. Her blunt ways did not measure up to his ideal of womanhood, either, and he'd brought her home early. She and Clara still made jokes about it.

How long are you going to be in the bathroom, Clara? *Shorter than a date with Dave.*

How far is it to Rose Garden Quilts from home, Patricia? *Shorter than a date with Dave.*

This morning, Patricia could feel the gazes of the women on her, though she kept her hands clasped in her lap and her gaze modestly down. She tried to focus on the preaching, but mostly she spent the three hours of the service coming up with replies to the questions she could feel hovering in the air of the big living room of the Keim ranch house on the K Bar K.

The fellowship meal of cold meats, cheeses, and trimmings for sandwiches was laid out on big trays, and there were big bowls full of as many potato chips and pickles and scoops of potato salad as your plate could hold. Patricia sat with her eldest brother Simeon and his intended, Susan Bontrager, on purpose. They were deep in plans for a wedding that was months away—not until after Christmas— but it was all Susan could talk about. That, and the house Sim was building on a nice piece of land he'd bought to the north of town.

Patricia was happy for her brother, truly. Susan might feel like a burr in your sock to most people, but her brisk, bossy ways and tendency to get things done before most people even got started suited Sim down to the ground. But Susan's unconscious protection didn't last once they'd all devoured the blueberry crumble and the lemon meringue pie that was Sylvia Keim's specialty. As people left the tables, Patricia looked around for another safe haven. Maybe outside.

"*Liewi*, come keep me company." As Patricia emerged onto the front porch, she looked to the left for the familiar voice. Aendi Annie Gingerich sat in the shade, rocking gently in the chair set out for her use. An afghan had been tossed over the back in case the breeze got chilly.

Her great-aunt was hardly ever alone. Patricia didn't waste the opportunity, just pulled up the stool that Annie wasn't using and settled next to her.

"I won't keep you long," Annie said. "A young girl like you should be with her friends."

"Not so young, Aendi. I turned twenty-one in the spring, remember?"

Annie chuckled. "Only the very young and the very old want to grow older. We old folks are as bad as little *Kinner*—I'm ninety-one and a half. Not ninety-one. Have to add that half, like I'm really accomplishing something."

"I'm just glad there is a half. And a two in January, and a three the January after that."

"That's up to the *gut Gott*, and no amount of optimism and green vegetables will change it." She used one foot to set the rocker in motion. "Is everything all right, *Liewi?*"

She must have heard. "*Ja, Aendi.*"

"I hear there was some excitement among the *Youngie* at Petersheims' Friday night."

"Calvin somehow overturned a pot of boiling strawberry taffy," she said, knowing perfectly well that wasn't what the elderly lady meant. "What a mess."

"Not quite the excitement I was referring to."

Patricia gave in. "Some people might have thought it was exciting. It was only Chance Madison, giving me a ride over there after I got off work."

"It's not the ride that set the cat among the pigeons so much as the *Englisch* boy joining in your doings. How did that come about?"

"Oh, I asked him." She glanced up, wondering if she'd see censure in the sharp old eyes, but Annie was gazing placidly across the home pasture to where the buggies were lined up along the fence. "I think he's lonely. He's a little different from his brothers—thank goodness—and I didn't have the heart to tell him to go away."

"Goodness is one of the fruits of the Spirit," Annie said mildly. "Though I understand longsuffering might have had a part in it, too. Something to do with taffy as well?"

Patricia had to smile. "He dropped it in the grass. The whole loaf. It was almost ready, too, and smelled so *gut*. But that was nothing to what Sarah Jane had to put up with. You should have seen her chase Calvin out of the kitchen—with a mop."

"I wish I had. He's been giving her a wide berth this morning. It was a blessing no one got burned." A pause, and then, "What about you? Is there no one among the *Youngie* who catches your eye?"

"*Neh*, not really."

"A lot of couples working toward creating homes for *Gott* to dwell in, these days," Annie mused. "Those boys of Rachel Miller's seem like nice young men."

"I suppose so. I hadn't noticed." Did it count if all you noticed was how irritating a man could be?

"Those cousins of the Keims there will be leaving after roundup," Annie went on, as if Patricia didn't know the date

Bethany and Sharon had to catch the train. "I wonder if that Mark Steiner is going to muster up the courage to ask one of them to stay."

"He's had plenty of time. It's not like their best-by date is going to expire the day after Labor Day."

"What about him?" As though he'd heard her, Mark walked past with both the Keim cousins, all three talking a mile a minute.

Patricia looked from him to Annie, startled. "Who? Mark?"

"Why not? He might not have succeeded with Sylvia and married into the ranch, but you could give those girls some competition."

Patricia had not given Mark Steiner more than a passing glance in all the time he'd been in the valley. He wasn't her type. None of the young men here were. Even if her idea of her type changed almost daily.

"Ach, well," Annie said. "You don't need to be seeing anyone to make your wedding quilt. Have you started it yet?"

Patricia laughed at the well-worn joke. "I bet you asked Mamm that when she was my age. And her *mamm* before that."

"I did ask my sister, and both Kate's sisters, too. It's tradition in our family, you know that."

"Tradition? Sure it's not more of a fairy tale? Because I'm not the swan princess sewing shirts for her brothers."

"I'm not talking about shirts, *Liewi*, though that is something we all do when we have men to look after. I'm talking about tradition. The same year you start your wedding quilt, *der Herr* will reveal the one He means for you by Christmas."

Surely Annie didn't believe that. Probably over the years, one or two of the aunts and great-aunts had started a quilt and met their future husband in the same year. That didn't make *Gott in Himmel* a party to what amounted to coincidence.

"*Der Herr* had better act quickly, then," she said flippantly. "It's already August."

"It's not Him that needs to act quickly," Annie said, "it's you. At least choose some fabrics while you're between customers at the quilt shop. Cut some fat quarters. That counts as a start."

"Do you want me married off so fast, Aendi?" she teased. "What happened to one day with the Lord being like a thousand years, and a thousand years as one day?"

"If we all had a thousand years, I wouldn't be talking to you like this," Annie said with mock sternness. "You mark my words. Start that quilt, and you'll see that I'm right."

"All right. I promise I will start something this coming week. Even if it's a pot holder."

Annie shook her head. "Has to be a quilt. A wedding quilt for your hope chest. Though it won't be in there long once you get it finished. You'll see. The women in our family call it a tradition for a reason."

Patricia got up and leaned over to kiss the soft, wrinkled cheek. "As it happens, I was looking at quilt patterns just the other day. You have to promise that when I get the top done, we'll have a quilting frolic close to Christmas so that one of us can stitch *I told you so* right into the border."

"That will be me," Annie said with the calm of absolute certainty.

Patricia couldn't help smiling as she walked down the porch steps and Sylvia Keim took her place on the stool. There would be a steady stream of people coming to talk to Aendi Annie after lunch—there always was. Patricia felt a glow of gratitude for the day that Annie had written to Mamm—her favorite niece—asking for help with her little farm, and offering the family the opportunity to take it over. Neither of her sons wanted it, but Dat had jumped at the offer, and before you could say *jackelope* they had moved up here from Kentucky, to the last place Patricia ever expected to be.

The most beautiful, and sometimes the most harsh place, but despite that, the Siksika had found its way into her heart.

As she joined Rose's daughters Julie and Beth Stolzfus under a stand of pines, careful not to lean on the trunk and get her dress covered in sweating pitch, she found herself looking forward to opening the shop on Tuesday morning. If none of the patterns in stock suited her, she'd sketch out that quilt in her head and then have the happy task of choosing all the fabrics that would make it a reality.

As for the family tradition, she didn't believe a word of it. But she'd do nearly anything for her great-aunt, and she hadn't made a queen-sized quilt in a while. Why shouldn't she make one for her hope chest? If *Gott* willed that she stay single, she could still enjoy sleeping under it herself.

Across the creek, Gideon Miller laughed at something Alden Stolzfus said and happened to glance in their direction.

Patricia turned her back on him. She wasn't a talented quilt designer like his cousin Malena, but the art of piecing and the fun of creating gave her joy. Which was more than she could say for any kind of attention from him.

GIDEON AND SETH HAD LONG AGO SQUARED IT WITH ONKEL Reuben that on Sundays, they were free to stay for the singing instead of heading home to do ranch chores. Granted, there were some seasons when this just wasn't practical, such as in the early spring when the cows were dropping their calves and every man was needed to check the snowy pastures and bring the weak and sickly animals into the barn. But on a sunny August day, Reuben was content to look after the animals himself. Tonight he and Aendi Naomi had been invited to enjoy a meal at Daniel's house overlooking the bends of the Siksika River, so that Aendi Naomi had a holiday from cooking.

So here he was, plunking himself down in front of a hymnbook on the boys' side of one of the half-dozen tables set up in the Keim living room. He picked up the book and looked up, to see that he'd managed to park his carcass directly opposite Patricia and Clara King.

How had he managed this? He'd meant to sit opposite Sharon Keim at the next table over, just to give Mark Steiner a hard time. Well, he was stuck now until after supper, when people tended to move around if they wanted to. Of all the bad luck.

Evidently he wasn't the only one thinking so, if the flash of horror he'd seen in Patricia's eyes was any indication. To give her credit, she covered it up quickly, and lowered her lashes to study the cover of the hymnbook as if she'd never seen it before.

"Gideon." Clara nodded at him. "Seth is still here, isn't he?"

"He'll be along. He's outside stalling Calvin until everyone gets a seat."

"It's safer that way," she agreed. "Someone needs to shake some sense into that boy. Poor Cathy Petersheim went home with her parents."

Just to avoid Calvin Yoder? "That's extreme."

"Desperate times call for desperate measures."

"He'll be chasing someone else by next church Sunday." Patricia sounded a little unwilling to join the conversation.

"Maybe even you." Gideon smiled at her. "But better him than Chance Madison."

Patricia's mouth dropped open as the breath seemed to huff out of her lungs. To his chagrin, her grey eyes filled with tears.

She abandoned her hymnbook, swung her feet over the bench, and headed for the kitchen door, swerving around Seth and Calvin as they came in. Calvin gazed after her as the door closed, then shrugged and lumbered over to take a spot at the end of one of the benches.

"That was unkind," Clara observed.

Before Gideon could defend himself, Sylvia, acting as hostess for probably the last time before she and his brother Tobias were married, announced the number of the first hymn. To give him credit, Calvin often acted as *Vorsinger* because he had lungs like a bellows and could carry a tune. He also sang them significantly faster than they ever sang in church, which Gideon appreciated. Much as he loved the slow Sunday singing from the *Ausbund*, it was fun to speed things up a little. And Calvin knew every one of the songs written in his sister's songbook, things like "Take Me Home, Country Roads" (which they only sang when the adults were out in the yard), "The Old Rugged Cross," and the ones written by an Amish girl out in Colorado, Cora Swarey, whose correspondence was probably huge from the number of *Youngie* writing to ask for copies of the songs she wrote.

When Patricia didn't come in by the time they began the second verse, he started to think maybe Clara was right. Maybe he shouldn't have needled her. He'd kind of meant it, even though no sane man would wish Calvin Yoder on any girl.

But it was perfectly true that an Amish man, no matter how clumsy and socially awkward, was better for an Amish girl than any *Englisch* man on the planet.

Maybe at supper he'd find her and apologize. Not for the truth of what he'd said, but for hurting her feelings in saying it. Mind you, he didn't know *why* her feelings had been hurt. But that didn't matter. He'd injured a sister in Christ, and it was his place to make it right.

 ❧　4　❧

PATRICIA STOOD by the fence that divided the ranch house's yard from the home pasture, where the horses cropped the grass as they waited placidly for the singing to be over. It wasn't often she got to hear the *Youngie* singing at a distance. She was always in the middle of it. But all at once, sitting opposite Gideon Miller had been more than she could bear.

So she'd been out here for long enough for the stars to prick out, simmering down and trying to decide if that man had actually meant to be insulting—imagine settling for Calvin Yoder!—or if he was just repeating what *obviously* she already knew. Of course an Amish man should be an Amish woman's choice. It wasn't her fault if some of the Amish men were clueless about how terrible a choice they were.

Poor Calvin. Though she could hear his voice from here. He liked singing, and had a surprisingly good voice, though of course it would never do to tell him so. He'd likely be the Sunday *Vorsinger* someday even if he never got married, and when the bishop asked him to render that service in church, it would be with the caution that he'd need to slow it down so the old folks could keep up.

She smiled at the thought, and patted Goldie's nose when the King buggy horse came up to the fence to see if she had a carrot in her pocket. Sadly, she didn't, but Goldie made do with affection. At length came the sound of dishes and food being placed on tables and Patricia sighed. "I'll see you later, girl," she told the horse. "I think I can go in now without being tempted to throw something."

"I'm glad to hear it," said a male voice several feet away. A voice she recognized instantly, even though she couldn't see him very well. It was fully dark now, though a glow in the sky told her the three-quarter moon would be rising over the mountain peaks any minute.

"Enschuldichung," she said, turning away as Gideon joined her at the fence.

"Don't go," he said. *"Bidde.* Your sister said something to me, and I want to apologize."

"Go apologize to her, then." She took a step away.

"Not to her." There was a note in his voice that could have been worry, or frustration. "To you. For saying what I said. I didn't mean to hurt your feelings, and I'm sorry for it."

She couldn't very well walk away now, though the shorter she kept this conversation, the better.

"Apology accepted." There. That would do. She would have gone, except curiosity made her hesitate. "What did Clara say?"

"That what I said was unkind. I didn't mean it that way."

Denki, Clara, for a word in season. "How did you mean it? That an Amish girl shouldn't go looking over the fence at *Englisch* men?"

He hesitated. "Something like that."

"Well, obviously. What you don't seem to realize is that you said something unkind about Calvin, too. He didn't hear it, but anyone around you could have. It's not his fault he's like a moose in the road at rush hour. He was born that way. It doesn't give people grounds to make jokes about him."

Where had all these words come from? She'd turned Calvin down when he'd asked to take her home, hadn't she? And now she was defending him?

"You're right," Gideon said unexpectedly. "Honestly, I think he does more damage to himself than anyone else."

"Sarah Jane might not agree."

"*Neh,*" he conceded. "I was looking forward to that strawberry taffy, too. Did you get it all off the floors?"

"We had lots of help. I guess you'll have to host a taffy pull at the Circle M. A rematch—because some of us never got to pull." She thought of Chance, trying to pick grass out of the hardening taffy, completely unaware of what else had been walking around the yard before he got there.

"That's a good idea. Or at the Inn. Mamm's always fully booked, but the guests might get a kick out of it. If we're inviting *Englisch* these days, they might even want to join in."

Despite his resigned tone, Patricia was warming to the idea. "The Inn is a lot closer than the Petersheim place. It would be fun. Though ... I suppose the Inn's guests are different from random Madisons and would be more welcome?"

He chuckled, and draped his arms on the fence. "At least they've paid to be there. Cookies and taffy are a bonus. Do you want me to ask Mamm? They're coming up to the Circle M for dinner on Wednesday, along with the bishop's family. Little Joe says he needs to straighten out his calendar. He's losing track of all the weddings."

"Sure, ask her. She doesn't have to do a thing—we can set up the volleyball net down by the barn, and the propane cooker out by the barbecue so that even if Calvin falls into the pot, it won't make a mess in the kitchen and force the guests to cut their holidays short."

"Maybe we should put a note on the website. *Caution: Watch for bear, moose, and Yoders.*"

She smiled in spite of herself. Because he wasn't being mean. He was poking gentle fun—and the truth was, Calvin would be the first one to laugh.

"That's a plan, then," Gideon said. "Coming in to supper?"

"Bye, Goldie," she said to the horse, in lieu of a reply. "Clara and I will be back soon."

Half an hour ago, if anyone had told her she'd be walking beside Gideon Miller without wanting to run away scream-ing, she'd have told them they needed to give their head a shake.

And yet, here she was.

Mind you, there was still time. There was a lot of the evening left yet.

11:15 p.m.

As she and Clara unhitched Goldie and rubbed her down, Patricia reflected that on the whole, the evening hadn't gone too badly. Even with Gideon Miller in it.

A lamp cast a golden light from the living room windows, but still, they went into the house as quietly as they could, and Clara vanished upstairs. She had the gift of being able to drop off to sleep right away, but after an evening out, Patricia liked to take her time, enjoying the quiet of a house that was always bustling with activity during the day. She filled a glass of water and wandered into the living room to find Dat in his easy chair, reading *The Budget*.

"*Gut* idea," he said, closing the Amish magazine. "Get me one?"

She handed him hers and went back to the kitchen to fill another for herself.

"Did you enjoy the singing?" he asked when she returned.

She nodded, making herself comfortable in her favorite corner of the sofa. "Poor Calvin is still in disgrace from Friday, but he redeemed himself a little by being *Vorsinger*."

"That boy inhabits a bigger world than everyone around him. Makes it hard to navigate."

Maybe that was one way of looking at it. "Some were talking about trying again with a taffy pull. Somewhere closer in."

"I hope they do. Speaking of Friday, I had a little visit this afternoon out by the buggies before I brought your mother and Aendi Annie home. With Paul Petersheim."

Any faint hopes Patricia might have had that her parents wouldn't have heard about who had taken her to the taffy pull vanished like liquid on a hot woodstove. She took a sip of water and waited.

"He was quite concerned." Dat took a sip, too. "About your arriving with that Madison boy."

She had to make this sound as harmless as possible. "He or someone else from the Rocking Diamond usually takes me into town on the days I work late. On Friday, Chance wasn't doing anything special, so he dropped in to ask if he could run me home after I cashed out."

"That was kind of him. Except you didn't come home."

"I wanted to go to the volleyball game and the taffy pull, so he took me over there instead."

Dat didn't answer, clearly waiting for her to get to the part that troubled him.

"He looked so lonely, Dat. I didn't have the heart to just send him on his way. So I asked if he'd like to join us for a while."

"And *Englisch* boy at Amish doings? That particular *Englisch* boy?"

"He's not like his brothers."

"We can be thankful for that. Paul told me there was an accident."

"Nothing that couldn't be cleaned up. A bunch of the girls helped Sarah Jane with the pot of taffy that went over in the kitchen."

"I think there's more to be cleaned up here than taffy, *Dochder*."

Patricia leaned forward, gripping the water glass in both hands. "It was nothing, Dat. He played some volleyball, dropped the taffy we were pulling, and went home."

"You were pulling with him?"

"It was boys and girls. He'd never done it before."

He gazed at her. The curtain at the window bellied out with the night breeze, then fell back.

"Honest, Dat. It was nothing. If he asks me again, I'll tell him no."

"I don't think you should give him the opportunity to ask again."

How? Put a hand over his mouth? "I'll do my best."

"I think you should do more than that. I think that tomor-row, you should give the Madisons a week's notice, and tell them you won't be working for them anymore."

Patricia's mouth fell open. "Quit my job?" Over inviting their son to a taffy pull?

"You have another one."

But Taylor Madison paid more than Rose Stolzfus. "They have a big group of businessmen coming next week. I can't leave now. Zefra is going to need every pair of hands she can get."

"Plenty of *Englisch* girls looking for work in the valley. It will be a *gut* opportunity for one of them."

"I'm already trained. Besides, what if I cause offense, just up and quitting?"

"I'm sure that if you are wise as a serpent and harmless as a dove, you won't."

"But I want to work there. I can't find a job that pays so well. You said that yourself when I applied. You *encouraged* me to apply."

"I did," he agreed. "But it never occurred to me that one of those boys would even notice you, never mind behave the way he did."

What did that mean? "You make it sound like he was out of line. He wasn't. He just gave me a ride to Petersheims'."

"I don't want you riding with any of them. Your sister will take you tomorrow morning in the buggy, then collect you at noon. On the days you work late at the quilt shop, she'll pick you up after work. And that will be that."

Clara was going to love having her orderly day turned upside down to cart Patricia all over creation, just because Paul Petersheim felt it necessary to tattle. When Patricia had done nothing wrong. When Chance had done nothing wrong, either, for goodness sake.

But Patricia couldn't disobey her father. She'd seen what had happened to her middle brother Andrew during his *Rumspringe* days—how Dat had tried to rein him in more and more tightly, and only succeeded in driving him away. Andrew had never been able to rule his spirit enough to submit to *Gottes wille*, the *Ordnung*, or their father, and as a result, it was months before they'd seen him again.

He'd taken off in a car with an *Englisch* girl the second time he'd left the fold. Maybe that was the trouble. Maybe Dat thought history was going to repeat itself.

Well, she wasn't Andrew, and he'd come back and stayed in church this time, once he'd met Kate Weaver's sister, and history was what you made it.

"All right, Dat." She rose and held out her hand for his empty glass.

But he didn't let it go right away. He hung on, his warm fingers covering hers. "It's for the best, *Liewi*," he said gently. "We'll find you another job if you feel you need one."

She could have said a lot of things. That she had found one she liked and that paid well, and suddenly it wasn't good enough. That jobs weren't so easy to come by here. That she was a grown woman and old enough to make her own decisions.

But she didn't. She only said evenly, "*Guder nacht*, Dat. Sleep well."

She washed the glasses. Brushed her teeth. Went up to her room across the hall from Clara's and hung up her dress. Put on her nightie and climbed into bed.

She didn't kneel to say her prayers. She was too angry. Instead, she lay there listening to Clara snore gently from the other side of the house, and replayed the whole conversation with her father, this time saying all the things that she'd wanted to.

Funny, though ... in the end she still didn't win.

5

THE CIRCLE M RANCH

Wednesday, August 10

GIDEON AND SETH got up pretty early as a rule; the animals needed care before anything else, and then it was on to whatever task was on Reuben's mind for the day. After seeing to the animals, they typically walked up to the big house for breakfast.

But today was a whirlwind of activity even greater than usual. The bishop's family was coming to dinner, along with Gideon's own family. Naomi, her daughters, and her daughters-in-law were already hard at work, and it was pretty likely Susanna would be along after all the Inn's guests were looked after. While Malena and Kate Weaver saw to breakfast, Naomi had already begun browning cubes of beef for what looked like stew.

Gideon hoped so. He loved stew. It wasn't his aunt's elk stew—that was reserved for roundup and Christmas—but her beef stew was still something to write home about. After a grace that was as silent as possible considering the sizzling and popping from the stove, he dug into his biscuits, bacon, and eggs with an appetite.

Naomi and Malena ate standing up, taking turns at the big cast-iron pans. Sitting next to her fiancé Adam, Kate finished her plate in half the time he did and got busy with the dishes.

"Where do you want us today, Onkel Reuben?" Seth asked, before biting into a fluffy biscuit running with butter. "We should be thinking about checking the collection pens up on the allotment, *nix*?"

"They can wait a day. You're needed right here," Reuben said. "Your aunt and the girls will be cooking up a feast, which means you'll be helping me wash the windows, raking up the yard, picking tomatoes—"

"*More* tomatoes," Kate groaned from the sink.

"—to take down to Lovina for canning, and doing any little job your aunt needs you to do."

A day spent close to where food was being prepared sounded pretty good to Gideon. As he, Seth, Adam, and Reuben prepared buckets and brushes for the windows, he spotted Ruby Wengerd, the bishop's daughter, coming down the shortcut that ran past Adam's house and out to the county highway. His cousin Zach met her at the bottom of the slope and took her hand as they walked toward the house.

Gideon smothered a smile. Zach wasn't about to kiss his intended right in front of his family, but from the glow in Ruby's face as she looked up at him, he might as well have. When he saw her into the house, he came out again with his First Aid backpack on.

"He caught day shift at the volunteer fire department today," Adam said to Gideon. "That was a stroke of luck. Means he should be home for dinner."

"At least long enough to settle his wedding date," Seth

said, setting the stepladder in front of the leftmost of the three big windows that framed the mountains in the living room.

"I'm pretty sure Little Joe and Ruby have already done that," Reuben said from the middle window, the corners of his mouth quirking up in a smile. "All that's left is for someone to tell Zach."

"If you want to know a secret—" Adam stopped. "*Neh*, I promised. We'll hear all about it at dinner." He went to work on the rightmost window as if to take himself away from temptation.

Gideon and Seth looked at one another and shrugged. There was no such thing as keeping a secret in this family. But if Adam was in on it, then maybe Zach was, too, and that might mean—

"Double wedding," Seth whispered under cover of climbing the ladder to start at the top of the window, while Gideon took the bottom half. "Just wait."

Wedding fever had run rampant on the ranch. There wasn't a single person unaffected by it—literally. There were no single people left on the Circle M. All his cousins were either married or soon to be. And their own branch of the family was well on its way to the same fate.

Maybe there was something in the water. That turquoise blue the Siksika River sometimes turned when the light was right was supposed to be from glacier melt, but maybe there was something more powerful going on.

"It's up to you and me to stay strong," he said to his brother, wielding brush and cloth with energy. "The bishop has to pace himself. It's our duty to help."

"For at least a year," Seth agreed. "Probably longer, considering the prospects in the valley."

"Come on. What about Cathy Petersheim? Or Sharon Keim? Beth Stolzfus?"

"You left out Julie."

"Julie is not your type. You don't play hockey, so she won't even look at you."

"What about *your* type?"

"I don't have one. I just hope *der Herr* sends me someone who's pretty, nice, and a good cook."

"That's a type. And every one of those girls you just mentioned fits it."

That was true. Except maybe Sharon. She seemed to be too busy flirting to spend much time in the kitchen.

"What about Patricia King?" Seth went on, busy scrubbing above his head. "I saw you two talking by the fence last night. Is the war over?"

Something about his brother's laughing tone rubbed Gideon the wrong way. "There isn't any war. She just doesn't like me. And I can't say I like her, either."

Reuben glanced over, but Gideon was pretty sure that with the *scritch* of brushes and the slosh of water, he hadn't heard him.

"She's practically family," Seth said. "Noah and Rebecca will be here tonight. But not her, I guess."

Thank goodness for that.

"If you boys are done ratchet-jawing," Reuben said, "you can leave that ladder with us. Get started on the windows on the back deck, and Adam and I will do the ones on the south side when we finish here. Then we'll move upstairs." Seth polished the big pane with vinegar and newspaper, and moved the ladder one window over. Then he and Gideon went around to the back, whose windows were just normal, not double height like the living room ones.

"I wonder if we'll have a house like this someday," Gideon said, getting busy with the brush.

"Not likely on a hand's pay. We'll have to do like Tobias did, and marry a woman coming into a ranch."

"I think Tobias had more than the ranch on his mind when he finally tumbled to the fact that he might lose Sylvia to Willard Zook."

"She was never going to marry him," Seth scoffed. "Anyway, Willard seems to have recovered, if the Zook buggy over at Rose's half the time means anything."

He'd have to ask Patricia what was going on th—

What is the matter with you? Since when are you going to ask Patricia anything, especially about her employer? That would involve actually speaking, and you've done enough of that for one week and escaped with your skin intact.

"It's finally happened," Gideon said with some gloom. "We have fallen to the level of our sister, and given in to gossip."

"Gossip is mean underneath. News isn't."

"That's what I like about you, *Bruder*. You have a different way of looking at the world."

Seth made a sound of derision in his throat. "And Susanna doesn't gossip. She's been the subject of it too often."

That was true enough.

There were plenty of other things to talk about, though, like the best way to get the upstairs windows clean, the collection pens on the allotment and what tools they'd need to take for repairs, whether Calvin Yoder should be allowed to come to the prospective taffy pull or if he should just be locked in the barn for safekeeping. Onkel Reuben had no shortage of jobs, and by the end of the day, the ranch house gleamed with cleanliness just as nicely as if church were to be held there the next day.

Gideon and Seth showered and changed and presented themselves to Aendi Naomi at five-thirty, just before the bishop and his family were expected. She gave them a critical glance up and down, then smiled. "You'll do." Then she glanced out the clean living-room window, where Rebecca was hovering, her baby sister Deborah in her arms. "Any sign?"

Rebecca shook her head. "Noah couldn't have forgotten. It was all we talked about at breakfast. Little Joe and Sadie will be here any minute."

Noah and Rebecca were living here until their house was finished. While Gideon knew he spent long hours working on it, sometimes even giving up paid jobs in order to complete the house before the snow flew, the responsible Noah would never be late for a family event if he could help it.

"Little Joe and Sadie will forgive him, even if he rolls in at midnight," Naomi said, taking the baby. "Time for this one to have her own dinner, hey, big girl? Don't fret, *Liewi. Dei Mann* will be home before long."

The words were hardly out of her mouth when Rebecca spotted their buggy in the distance across the home fields, where there weren't many trees to obscure the view. She breathed a sigh of relief, one hand to her chest. Just in time, too, for the bishop and his wife came around the final bend in the lane, enjoying a summer afternoon's walk hand in hand. Under the other arm the bishop carried the eight by eleven hardcover calendar that recorded the dates and doings of everyone in both church districts.

Behind them were Joshua and Sara Miller in their buggy, their little boy Nathan on her lap.

It didn't take long for the house to fill up. Mamm and Luke rolled in, bringing Susanna and Stephen, while Tobias, his fiancée Sylvia, and his twins Gracie and Benny followed in

Tobias's family buggy. Of course the twins had to greet every single horse in the pasture, the chickens in the yard, and the barn cats. Then they insisted that Gideon show them the calf with the pulled tendon that Reuben had been nursing in the barn for nearly a week.

The twins were a handful, but Gideon couldn't imagine life without them. When he first heard that Tobias was going to be working on the K Bar K Ranch, he'd thought for sure and certain one of the boy-crazy cousins would have nabbed him and the twins, too. But it was quiet, gentle Sylvia with the core of steel who had stolen his heart. And now the twins would have a mother who loved them before her vows were even said, and Tobias would know the blessing of a loving marriage a second time.

Gideon couldn't imagine marriage for the first time. Oh, he'd dated a few girls, but it never came to much. Ranch hands tended to move around to where they were needed, even if that meant another state or county. Unless you were a foreman, assigned living quarters of your own, it wasn't fair to drag a woman from trailer to cabin to bunkhouse and expect her to try to make a home.

The tables had been set up the way they'd been at Christmas, with the furniture pushed back and two big dining tables pushed together. At one end was the children's table, where Sara would probably preside, as she'd done then. When the twins ran up the steps to see Reuben and Naomi, Gideon lingered in the yard waiting for Noah with an offer of help to unhitch and turn out his horse with the others.

Soon the buggy emerged from the lane, and Noah waved. Gideon waved back, and then peered more closely at the buggy. There was a woman next to Noah. He did a fast roll call in his head. Everyone was already here. Then who was—

"Whoa." Noah backed the buggy into the barn, set the brake, and hopped out. "Look who I found."

Zach emerged from the back of it, pulling his emergency kit with him. "Thanks for the lift, *Bruder*," he said cheerfully. "I'd have been late for Mamm's stew if it hadn't been for you."

He loped across the yard to the steps up to the house, but Gideon wasn't paying attention.

Patricia King slid out the passenger door, her face a mixture of politeness and chagrin. "I hope you don't mind my barging in," she said to Gideon. "Clara got held up and Dat asked Noah to pick me up in town on his way home, but there wasn't time to take me all the way out to the farm."

"I'm with Zach," Noah said cheerfully, working on the harness buckles. "Nothing is getting between me and your aunt's beef stew."

Gideon moved to the other side of the horse, his fingers moving automatically on the buckles while his brain adjusted to the sight of the last person he expected to join them. "You're welcome here anytime," he said, gathering his manners up like a bunch of dropped firewood. "They'll be glad to see you up at the house."

"Denki," she said, and headed across the yard.

Well, he supposed Noah's sister was close enough to family to make no difference. And hospitality was built into the Circle M, right from its spacious, welcoming rooms to the attitude of everyone in the house. Even little Deborah lit up like a candle when company came in the door. She wasn't even two and already she had the red hair and the outlook of her big sister Malena, who had never met a stranger.

Gideon figured he was probably the only one on the whole place who was less than happy about the extra guest. Not because he begrudged her a place at the table. It wasn't even his table. But because the ease and familiarity of being with his family now had a hitch in it. He wouldn't be as free to speak and joke and laugh now. He'd always be wondering what she thought, what she felt, whether she'd go home and think over the evening at all.

Get a grip. Why do you care what she thinks?

But there was no answer to that question.

6

PATRICIA HAD BEEN to the Circle M for supper a number of times, in addition, of course, to the fellowship meal after church. The big living room, designed to accommodate all the families from the west district, was alive now with chatter and laughter, though the clatter of forks on plates was slowing. Her own waistband was uncomfortably tight after the pie, and she was giving serious consideration to unfastening just one snap under cover of her apron.

But exercise might be a better idea. She jumped up to help clear the table, leaving an especially wide space in front of Little Joe. He and Sadie were seated at about the halfway point so that he could see everyone who was causing such confusion in the big black book.

"We'll do the dishes after," Malena whispered. "While Mamm serves coffee."

"Are you and Alden getting a date tonight?" Patricia whispered back.

Malena looked both thoughtful and innocent. "I guess he might consider dinner away from home a date."

"Oh, ha ha. Very funny."

Malena only smiled and refused to say more. But her eyes were sparkling as they hurried out to their places at the table.

"All right, then," Little Joe boomed, opening the calendar and pulling a newly sharpened pencil out of a loop on the side. "Let's see where we are."

Patricia was dying to get a look at it, but probably the only person allowed to peruse all those pencilled-in scribbles and notations was Sadie Wengerd. Usually weddings were announced a few weeks before they happened—as if the entire *Gmay* didn't already know. Back east, people tended to keep a close watch on the vegetable gardens, looking for the telltale presence of celery. It was tradition to include it in the wedding feast, whether tucked into jars on the table, or in hot dishes where it was creamed.

But celery didn't grow very well in the Siksika—the growing season was too short, and even if you started seeds in a greenhouse, a late frost or a blizzard like the one a few weeks ago would kill off the whole crop, valley-wide. But if one traditional dish was missing, no one seemed to pine for it. There were too many others, like *roascht*, Gideon's personal favorite.

Little Joe turned pages until he arrived at October. He put his reading glasses on his nose. "Luke Hertzler and Rachel Miller, October fourth, at Willard and Zeke's place. It's early in the season, so no confusion there."

"Right in the middle, between the fishermen leaving the Inn and the elk hunters arriving," Gideon explained to Noah on his other side, just audibly enough for everyone to hear.

Rachel smiled into the eyes of her intended, and Luke gazed back as though she were the sun and the moon rolled into one.

"The following Tuesday, the eleventh, Stephen Kurtz and Susanna Miller, at the Inn."

Patricia felt a jolt of surprise. She hadn't known their wedding was even being thought of this year. But then, while Stephen hadn't been in the valley all that long, he'd been foreman on their ranch in New Mexico. So they'd known each other for some time ... off and on.

Little Joe looked over his reading glasses at Tobias Miller. "You and Sylvia have anything you'd like to tell me? Now would be the time."

Sylvia blushed scarlet while down at the chldren's table, Gracie bounced to her feet before her father could gather himself to reply. "He proposed, Bishop!" she announced. "And Sylvia said yes!"

Poor Sylvia looked as though she wanted to slide bonelessly under the table.

"I'm glad to hear it," Little Joe said solemnly. "Did your father happen to mention a date?"

"Soon, he said," the little girl confided. "How soon does *soon* mean?"

"Gracie, *genug*," Tobias finally got out, now red in the face as well. Gracie wriggled back into her chair, apparently undaunted. "Bishop, we were going to come visit you, but— Well, we—we'd like an early date. Before school starts."

Consternation broke out around the table. "Before Labor Day? Before *roundup*?"

"We'll all be out on the allotments."

"The ranchers are going to be preparing."

"The whole church?"

"How are Josiah and Kathryn going to manage roundup *and* a wedding?"

Little Joe waited until the hubbub died down. "What day did you have in mind?" he asked Tobias.

"We thought about August thirtieth."

"Less than three weeks away?" Little Joe finally lost his calm.

The only people around the huge table who weren't bug-eyed or shaking their heads were Tobias and Sylvia. "I know it's unusual," Tobias said. "But with Josiah's nephews coming back from Colorado next week, plus any extra hands who come in for roundup, Benny won't be able to stay in the Bar K bunkhouse much longer. On the other hand, the schoolhouse is within walking distance of the Inn. Sylvia and I and the twins will live there with Mamm and Luke, and I'll simply ride to the K Bar K each day."

Little Joe gazed at him. "You've got this all figured out. The only thing you haven't yet accounted for is the others among the *Gmay* who will be busy at roundup."

Sylvia glanced at her intended, who nodded at the unspoken message. "This is my second marriage. I don't expect everyone in the *Gmay* to come, as they likely will for Susanna and Stephen after the cattle have all gone to market. If we have a family wedding at Keims' and keep it pretty small, it won't affect the work of the other ranchers. I know they'll understand."

Luckily the Keims had had church pretty recently, so the house and barns were probably still clean enough. Still, Patricia figured there would be some pretty frantic work frolics between now and then.

"And Josiah and Kathryn have agreed to this?"

Sylvia nodded. "We spoke to them, and they said that if you agreed, then they'd take on the extra work. Sharon and Beth will put off their return home by a week in order to help."

"They wanted to stay for roundup anyway," Susanna said. "Now they have a good reason."

Shaking his head, Little Joe flipped back a couple of pages and wrote their names in the square at the end of August.

Three weeks away. Patricia could hardly get her imagination around the frantic hive of activity the K Bar K was about to become.

You could hire on as a Maud. They need every pair of hands, and you could start after your last day on the Rocking Diamond.

If Josiah was hiring. If he wasn't beating the bushes for extra hands to ride the allotments while Kathryn, Sylvia and the girls were busy cooking and cleaning.

"*Denki*, Bishop," Tobias said, and let out a long breath. Maybe he thought their proposed date might have been refused. It very well could have been. A wedding at roundup! Patricia had only lived in the Siksika for a year or so, but even she knew the two major events of the cattlemen's year—the other one being spring turnout.

"That's the Millers from the Inn settled," Little Joe said. "I thought my own *Dochder's* wedding needed to be untangled, but hers is pretty straightforward in comparison to a wedding three weeks from now. Zachary, have you come to a decision after our visit the other night?"

Zach Miller took Ruby Wengerd's hand and held it tightly. "We talked it over, and we decided that while a double wedding in November would be fun—"

"For us, maybe," Adam said with a laugh. "I don't know about everyone else doing twice as much work."

"We thought we'd better wait until spring breakup. Noah tells me we could have my house done by then, and I can welcome my bride into her new home on our wedding day."

Patricia had never heard the bishop's daughter say more

than two sentences in public—she was the shyest person Patricia had ever met. But her face as she smiled into Zach's eyes spoke volumes about how much she loved him and how she couldn't wait for that day.

"But you could marry and live here," Naomi protested. "Just as Noah and Rebecca have been doing. Now that they're starting the finish work on their house, it won't be long before we have more empty bedrooms than full ones."

"I know, Mamm," Zach said, "and I'm grateful that you said so. If something goes wrong and the house can't be finished in time, then it's *gut* to know we have a backup plan. But I want to work toward our home if I can."

"Of course you do," Naomi said softly. "And I think you should."

"You'll come to me again in January, then, Zachary?" the bishop asked him, making a note in the lined pages in the back of the book. "You should have a better idea by then."

"*Ja*, Bishop. Ruby and I should be able to tell you right after New Year's."

That left Adam and Kate Weaver, across from Gideon at the other end of the table. "Is November seventeenth open in your book?" Adam asked, taking Kate's hand.

Pages flipped, and silence fell while Little Joe perused the squares. The thing about November and December was that these were the prime months for weddings. Not only here, but in most of the Amish communities Patricia had ever been to. Kate seemed to be holding her breath.

Little Joe shook his head. "*Neh*, nor the fifteenth either. And Thanksgiving week only has the Tuesday, and it's booked."

That was interesting. Weddings usually happened on Tuesdays and Thursdays, leaving time for the bench wagon to get from one wedding location to the next. And no one would ever get married on a Saturday, not with church the next day. The preparation for the latter was nearly as all-consuming as the former, both of them taking weeks.

Who in the valley had booked that date in the bishop's big calendar? What if it was Simeon and Susan? Well, they could certainly keep a secret, couldn't they? Patricia didn't think Mamm and Dat even knew, if she and Clara didn't. Ooh, wasn't she going to grill Simeon like a fish when she got home!

The bishop looked across at the young couple, who were beginning to look a little desperate. "The only date I have in November is the tenth. If that doesn't suit you, we'll need to look at December."

"We'll take it," Adam blurted without hesitation.

"It suits us down to the ground," Kate said. "Well before Thanksgiving, and we might be lucky enough to avoid some snow."

"Three months, and your house will be finished," Noah chimed in. "The timing couldn't be better."

Adam and Kate sat back, still holding hands, their faces wreathed in smiles. Patricia could feel their relief and happiness from here at having the all-important decision made. Now Kate and all the women on the Circle M could get busy with planning, and Kate would have the fun of choosing colors and deciding on invitations. Her family from Whinburg Township would travel to be here, including that sister who kicked up such a fuss over Adam last year. That sister who was dating Andrew now. Such a hubbub there would be, and when it was all over, the folks here on the ranch would take a nice break over Christmas while the newlyweds traveled back to Whinburg Township to make their honeymoon visits.

Patricia almost sighed, before she caught herself. Never mind. *She* didn't want to get married. Not just yet. In fact, a little idea that had been fluttering around in her head, peeking out at inconvenient moments, was becoming more and more of a certainty.

Which she wasn't about to blab here, of all places. That wouldn't be fitting, when these families had come together on purpose to talk about weddings.

The bishop looked around the table. "Anyone else, while I've got the book open?" he joked.

The room broke out in laughter. Patricia dared a glance at Alden Stolzfus, who had flushed so deeply it must have hurt. A couple of places away, Malena's blush clashed with her red hair and her burgundy dress until she looked as though she had caught fire. Since they weren't engaged and thus not sitting next to each other, they couldn't even take each other's hand for moral support.

Patricia found herself slouching down in her seat in sympathetic embarrassment.

And then Alden pushed back his chair and rose to his feet, the color still high in his cheeks. The laughter trickled into a confused and slightly astonished silence. He approached Malena's chair and held out his hand.

Were they leaving? Had he been so offended by a harmless quip that he was going home? Oh goodness, what would the bishop do?

Patricia could hardly breathe as Malena, looking as confused as Patricia felt, rose also.

And then Alden took her other hand in his, and gazed into eyes that were widening with realization.

"Malena," he said, "I'm a man who doesn't like to make a fuss, who doesn't stand out, who really believes in that old saying about every blade of grass making the meadow green. I'm a blade of grass. You're a glacier lily, as hardy as you are graceful, and blessed with so many gifts from *Gott* that I know I haven't seen half of them."

If it were possible to blush an even deeper shade, Malena did.

Naomi Miller gulped and pressed a hand to her mouth, her eyes filling with tears.

"But sometimes all a man can do is stand up and stand out, right in front of nearly everyone who matters to him. I'm sorry I didn't plan ahead so we could have Mamm and the girls here, too, but ..." He clasped her hands to his chest and gazed into her eyes. They could have been completely alone as a tear trickled down her cheek. "Malena Miller, will you be my wife? Will you make a home with me where the Spirit can live, and raise a family with me to love the Lord?"

Her mouth moved, but no sound came out. She tried again, and this time it worked. *"Ja,"* she said hoarsely. "I love you, Alden Stolzfus, and I will marry you, and I think we'd better get one of those dates before the bishop goes home with his book."

Laughter and tears broke out as Alden beamed and Naomi and Rachel hunted in their aprons for tissues until Sara reached over to offer a packet from Nathan's baby bag.

The bishop picked up his pencil once more and in less than a minute—Alden and Malena clearly being a couple who could make life-changing decisions without a fuss—the square for the twelfth of January had two new names written into it.

❦　7　❦

COFFEE AND DESSERT turned into an engagement party, with Sara, Rebecca, and Kate doing the honors. Naomi and Reuben took Alden and Malena off to the sofa, where Patricia couldn't hear what was being said, but Naomi and Malena's tears of happiness seemed to tell the story all too well.

Belatedly, Patricia remembered that someone was supposed to be doing the dishes, so she did her best to enjoy every bite of her applesauce spice cake with caramel frosting while hustling it down as fast as she could.

To her surprise, after a few minutes Gideon Miller joined her in the kitchen. If he wanted something other than coffee and cake, she couldn't help him, being up to her elbows in hot, soapy water, and she told him so.

"One piece of cake is enough," he said mildly, took a dish towel from the rack, and got busy drying the host of drinking glasses.

Goodness. Well, she wasn't about to complain. If the man wanted to dry dishes, it was a free country. When the glasses were washed, she got started on the dinner plates, and still there was no sound in the kitchen but swishing and clinking, and conversation and laughter from the living room.

Gideon reached up into the cupboard to put the glasses away. Clearly he knew his way around this kitchen. "I got a chance to ask Mamm if we could have a volleyball game at the Inn on Friday, and another try at a taffy pull. She said yes."

Half of Patricia was surprised that he hadn't forgotten. The other half was already figuring out how to let everyone know on such short notice. "Are you hosting? Do you have a cell phone?"

"Susanna and Stephen said they would, and Stephen does. I guess the *Youngie* will have something else to celebrate, what with Malena and Alden."

"I wish Rose and the girls could have been here. I wonder if they even know yet."

He chuckled and picked up a dinner plate. "I don't think even Alden knew until the moment the bishop made his joke."

"He sure has changed," Patricia said, scrubbing energetically. "When we first moved here, you never noticed him in a crowd. The only time you'd ever actually know Alden Stolzfus was there was if you were paying him to shoe a horse or build a gate."

"And now here he is, proposing to a woman in front of the bishop and a room full of people. I never would have believed it if I hadn't been right there at the table. Julie and Beth won't believe it, either."

It would be fun to listen in on that conversation, though.

"Speaking of unbelievable," he said, "is it true that Calvin Yoder asked Susan Bontrager's younger sister if he could take her home from singing next week?"

"I wouldn't know."

"Well, Susan is dating your brother, isn't she?"

Everyone knew that. "She and Simeon don't sit around the table talking about who is seeing whom. Besides, Leah's only eighteen, and I thought she was on *Rumspringe*. Calvin's been baptized—not exactly *Rumspringe* material. Or any material, come to that."

"And you'd know who was *Rumspringe* material? You've been baptized, too. So have I."

The nerve of him. He made her sound as though she was as old and staid as—as he was. "As it happens," she said, starting on the serving bowls, "I haven't been. Not yet."

"You're not baptized?" He stared at her, the plate in his hand frozen two inches above the others in the stack.

"Have you seen me in Communion lately?" Those who weren't baptized were always excused from the latter part of that service, which was for church members only.

"*Neh ... ja ...* huh. I don't remember."

"Well, you didn't. And I've decided that for the rest of the summer, I'm going to enjoy a little *Rumspringe* myself."

He put the plate on the stack so carelessly it was a wonder it didn't crack clear across. "Aren't you a little old for that? How do your parents feel about it?"

Good grief. Could he be any more insulting? "You just contradicted yourself, Gideon. Either I'm too old, or my parents have a say. Which is it?"

He flushed, and turned away to the cupboard as though he didn't want her to see. "I'm sorry. I didn't mean it that way. I just meant—well, people usually go on *Rumspringe* when they're Leah's age. Teenagers. Not people in their twenties."

"You know as well as I do that if you haven't joined church, it's an option," she said crisply. "And *neh*, I haven't told them. Sim didn't really bother with it, but both Andrew and Noah did. Even Clara did, for a month or two. Why shouldn't I?"

Maybe she shouldn't have mentioned Andrew, who was probably the poster child for the more dangerous side of dabbling in the world. But she wasn't Andrew—vain, self-absorbed, and more concerned about what image he was projecting to the world than actually being that person inside.

Gideon seemed to have forgotten the plates.

"Are you going to put those away?"

He looked at them as if surprised to see them stacked there, then picked them up and put one stack after the other into their cupboard.

He picked up a serving bowl, but didn't dry it. Instead, his mouth worked as though he were arranging words in his head. "Patricia," he said at last, "please listen. I have no right to tell you what to do—"

"I'd say not."

"—but as a brother, as almost a cousin-in-law—"

"Is that a thing?"

"—I'm hoping that you decide not to do this."

If she scrubbed the mixing bowl any harder, its painted surface would come off. She controlled her temper and gently swished the bowl in the rinse water, then set it in the drain rack.

"First," she said, resting her wrists on the sink and looking him in the eye for the first time, "You're right—only my parents have the right to tell me what to do."

"I know that, but as a friend—"

"Second, you don't know me. You've only been in the valley since February. It's not exactly a den of iniquity around here, if that's what you're afraid of."

"I didn't—"

"Third, I think my parents have brought me up well enough that even if I did choose to put on jeans and go out drinking and dancing—" The breath rushed out of him in what looked like horror, and she went on before he could recover. "—I'd still use the brain *Gott* gave me and not do anything as dangerous and stupid as you're clearly thinking."

"But you rode in Chance Madison's truck. At night. You brought him to a get-together."

"Oh, how dangerous *and* stupid of me!" she mocked.

So Chance Madison was the reason behind this sudden urge to act like her big brother. Well, she already had three of those. She didn't need another, sticking his nose in where it didn't belong. Judging her for something she hadn't even done. The nerve of him!

"I never thought you were stupid. I'm just trying to help."

"I don't need your help. In fact—"

"I thought I heard voices in here." Rebecca came into the kitchen, slipped an arm around Patricia's waist, and gave her a squeeze. "What a happy night—no one should be stuck in the kitchen. Want me to take over from one of you?"

"Sure," Gideon said in a low voice. "You'll need another dish towel. This one's soaked."

And to Patricia's enormous relief, he went out into the living room, leaving her with someone she actually liked. Then she realized something as Rebecca picked up a fresh towel and took his place.

Rebecca picked up a dripping bowl and tilted her head. "What? Do I have frosting on my cheek? It wouldn't surprise me. I wanted to dive face first into that cake. It's one of my favorites."

Patricia smiled at the picture. "*Neh*, no frosting. I just noticed that your eyes are the exact same color as Gideon's. Cornflower blue."

Rebecca nodded. "Malena's are, too. Not surprising, since

our fathers were brothers. What were you and Gideon talking about so seriously?"

"Friday night," she said. Well, it was true. "He wants to have a do-over for the taffy pull at the Inn. Hopefully there will be no accidents this time."

Rebecca raised an eyebrow. "Make sure and certain you ask for the help of *Himmel* with that one."

THE BISHOP WALKED HOME WITH HIS FAMILY, ZACHARY keeping them company. Patricia squeezed into Tobias and Sylvia's buggy, in the back with the *Kinner*, since the King place wasn't much out of their way back to the K Bar K. The rest of the family from the Inn and the Circle M went their various ways, and the quiet that followed a crowd's departure descended over the big house.

Seth headed out to the bunkhouse for bed, but Gideon was too restless. He wandered outside onto the porch, but that was as far as he got. The night was so still he could hear the river whispering beyond the barn and corrals. Maybe a walk along the bank in the cool night air would do him good.

He set off, cutting through the barn to the gate that led to the well-worn path. But before he got there, Noah stuck his head up from Hester the buggy horse's stall. "Gideon? Is that you?"

"*Ja*. Thought I'd take a walk."

"Need some time to clear your head after all the excitement?"

"You could say so."

"Mind if I join you?"

It was almost as if *Gott* had heard the jangle of his thoughts and sent a solution. He'd be a fool to turn it down. "Not a bit. You might even need the same."

"That I do." He patted the horse's rump and the two of them let themselves out into the lane that led down to the river path. "I was just giving Hester some extra oats. She had a busy day."

"I think we all did. But it was worth it. I've never been to an occasion like this. Usually when people get engaged and go to see the bishop, no one knows about it but him."

Noah chuckled. "There isn't much you could call *usual* about this family." From his tone, that was a plus, not a minus. "Though I have to say that Alden's proposing to Malena in front of her whole family was definitely unusual."

"That took courage."

"And the kind of love— What's that new song by Cora Swarey that's going around? Rebecca was singing it the other day."

"Kate, too. *The kind of love that never falters?*"

"That's the one." Noah shook his head. "That's Alden, through and through."

"Maybe someone ought to suggest to Malena that they sing it at their wedding, in the afternoon."

"I think you'll have more than enough someones making that suggestion," Noah said. "It was practically written for the purpose."

They emerged onto the path, and the air felt *gut* on Gideon's burning face. The full moon was climbing into the notch in the peaks, but at least moonlight didn't show a man blushing when he talked about love. He waited until they'd ambled far enough around the river's first bend to be pretty sure they couldn't be heard through any open windows up at the house, and gathered up his own courage.

"Noah, mind if I talk with you about something?"

"Not at all. I'm pretty sure the trout are asleep, and I'm not one to break a confidence. What's on your mind?"

Under this straightforward approach, all Gideon's half-formed sentences and roundabout lead-ups to the subject scattered just like those trout.

"It's about ... your sister," he blurted.

"Rebecca said she found you and Patricia in the kitchen having what sounded like a serious conversation."

Gideon tried to collect himself. "*I* was having a serious conversation. *She* was having an argument."

"Patricia? My even-tempered sister who never says a cross word to anyone?" Noah laughed at his own joke. "What about?"

"She wants a *Rumspringe*."

Noah's stride hitched, and after a moment, he waved at the bench on the riverbank ahead. "Let's sit."

Onkel Reuben had cut the bench from a chunk of Douglas fir specifically so that he could enjoy the view of the river with Aendi Naomi. It was sanded and varnished, its L-angle surprisingly comfortable. He and Noah settled onto it.

"My sister is twenty-one," Noah said. "She's an adult. Seems like she'd be thinking about joining church, not running around, at this late date."

"Which is pretty much what I told her. *Rumspringe* is for teenagers."

Noah was silent a moment. "Or people who think they're missing out on something. Did she say what brought this on?"

Gideon shook his head. "Has she ever mentioned it to the family?"

"*Neh*. Mamm and Dat are pretty much expecting her to ask about baptism classes any day now."

A couple of events connected themselves in Gideon's mind and formed a certainty. "I wonder if it has to do with the Madisons."

"If it does, it won't for long. Dat told her to hand in her notice. Her last day is Friday."

"Is that so?" It hadn't taken long for Arlon King to get wind of what had happened at the taffy pull. "Because of Chance giving her a ride to Petersheims'?"

"It's one thing to give an Amish girl who works for you a ride to her other job if you happen to be going to town. It's a whole other thing to wait for her to finish work—after dark—and offer her a ride home. Dat put his foot down."

A horrible thought occurred to Gideon, and he blurted it out without thinking. "You don't think she wanted to be alone with Chance, do you?"

"I have no idea. I hope not." He paused. "Is this what made you argue tonight?"

"I wasn't arguing. I just asked her not to do it. Go on *Rumspringe*. I didn't say anything about accepting rides with single *Englisch* men."

"And that did not go over well."

"It sure didn't."

Noah glanced sideways at him. "I don't know if you're really brave or a complete *Dummkopf*. You must have known it wasn't your place."

"I had to speak up. As a—a brother in Christ. But ... while we're friendly, like I am with all the *Youngie*, I don't think she considers me a friend."

"Probably not now," Noah agreed.

Well, he'd wanted honesty, hadn't he? Time for some of his own. "I messed it up," he said morosely. "But maybe you can talk to her about not doing it? If nothing else, encourage her to think it over some more?"

With a sigh, Noah said, "Here's the thing. Even when she was little, it was hard to tell Patricia anything. She always wanted to do things herself. Not to be obstinate, but to prove that what you said was true. If you told her not to lick the bar gate in January, without telling her why, she'd go do it just to see why you'd forbidden it."

"Ouch."

"At least she didn't blame me for that one. I don't think she's gotten over the combine incident. Mind you, it was Andrew's fault."

That didn't sound good. "What happened?"

"It was harvest, and kids being kids, we couldn't resist climbing up into one of those big combines the *Englisch* crew brought, just to see what the world looked like from up there. Andrew told her not to push the gear shift, but not what would happen if she did."

"Ouch times two."

"We got rolling for about twenty feet before one of the crew noticed the combine was moving, and oh boy, wasn't there a commotion. When Dat got done with us, not one of us could feel our behinds for a week."

He could only imagine. A bunch of Amish kids and a big, expensive, dangerous combine was an explosive combination. It was lucky none of them had been killed.

"I can try to talk to her when Rebecca and I are over to Kings' on Sunday," Noah said at last. "And I'll keep you out of it. But don't expect miracles."

"*Denki*, Noah. I'm just worried about her, is all. It's not like —" *I'm interested in her or anything.* He managed to stop himself before that part came out.

70

"Not like you're family," Noah supplied. "I know. But everyone needs a friend looking out for them, *nix?*"

He nodded, tried to smile, and got to his feet instead. "I guess we'd better head back. The work won't wait just because I've had a late night."

"You mean Reuben won't wait."

It felt *gut* to laugh. Gideon felt as though he hadn't been able to crack a smile since Patricia had turned her back on him and walked out of the kitchen.

❧ 8 ❧

THE ROCKING DIAMOND RANCH

Thursday morning, August 11

PATRICIA STRIPPED the king-sized bed in Cabin One with the ease of long practice. The sheets that Taylor Madison used in all the guest rooms felt cool and slippery—a contrast to the ones at the Wild Rose Amish Inn, which were a soft flannel. Montana nights were not exactly sultry, even in the summer, and Patricia and Clara both preferred flannel with a quilt. As Clara very practically said, it was easier to kick off the covers than ransack the linen closet to locate an extra blanket in the dark.

But apparently the guests at the Rocking Diamond liked their sheets elegant rather than cozy. Zefra had a particular way of tucking in the ends, so Patricia did that, then shook out the microfleece blanket and then laid what Zefra called *the duvet* over both. Nothing so homey as an Amish quilt here. The duvets were all a misty grey to match the towels and bath-room accessories.

Once the bathroom was cleaned, she vacuumed the cabin

and refreshed the snack bowl—also misty grey porcelain—and the mini fridge. She was just putting her cleaners and cloths back into their spaces in the cart when the door opened.

Expecting one of the other housekeeping staff looking to borrow something, Patricia nearly dropped her rag as Zefra's boss, Taylor Madison, stepped into the room. Even more ominous, she closed the door and ran an assessing gaze over Patricia's work.

She'd never done this before. Zefra usually checked all the cabins and rooms, giving each of them a homey touch with a single flower in a bud vase on the table. That was the signal that the work had been done to her exacting standards.

"Good morning, Mrs Madison," Patricia said. She wanted to ask if everything was in order, but she knew it was. The only thing out of order was that she wouldn't be working here after tomorrow.

"Good morning, Patty." A little silence fell, in which Patricia did her best not to fidget. Taylor Madison's blond hair was tied back in a sleek ponytail, and she wore a snap-front linen shirt with a yellow silk scarf at her throat. Her jeans and Tony Lamas were clean as a whistle. Patricia was pretty sure the woman knew how to get dirty, and rope and ride as well as her sons, but she'd never seen her do it. She'd only heard about Miss State Rodeo 2004 and seen the picture of her barrel racing in the bookcase in Mr Madison's study.

"Is there something I can do for you?" she finally ventured.

Mrs Madison turned that blue gaze on her. "Yes, there is. You can rescind your notice and stay on."

Taken aback, it was a little minute before Patricia could figure out what to say. "I can't do that. My father doesn't want me working here anymore."

"Is that so? Why didn't you say so when you spoke to Zefra?"

"I didn't want to," she said awkwardly. "I thought she might take offense."

"She didn't, but I surely did. I'm over it, but I'd like you to tell me why your father has a problem with us."

This woman was even more blunt than Clara, and that was saying something. Still, she wasn't about to tell her what she wanted to know. "I don't think it's you so much. If I have to have a second job, he wants me closer to home, that's all."

"We're closer to your place than the quilt shop."

Patricia flushed. "I think it's more in the sense of being Amish. A job closer to our ways."

"Don't you folks make beds and clean rooms?"

Patricia's heart began to pound as though she were about to run. Was this how a deer felt when it scented hunters? "Of course, but you know what I mean."

"I wish I did, Patty. I feel you're hiding the real reason from me, and I want to know what it is so I can fix it."

"My father's mind is made up. Once he does, there's no fixing it."

"I think there's more to it than that. You're dancing around the reason so hard you're practically out of breath."

"I'm sorr—"

"Does this have something to do with my son Chance?"

Patricia would have abandoned her cart and fled, but Mrs Madison was leaning on the closed cabin door. Other than going headfirst out the bathroom window and scattering all the lotions in the tray on the windowsill in the attempt, she was trapped.

"It's not his fault," she whispered.

"What isn't?" Those eyes had taken on an intensity you could almost feel, like the heat of a stove.

"He was only being nice. He stopped by after work at the quilt shop on Friday and offered me a ride home."

"And this made your father tell you to quit?"

"Partly. I was going to a—to some friends', not home, so Chance drove me over there. Like I said, he was being kind. Then he looked as though he wanted to join us, so I invited him. We—" A flash of inspiration hit. "They were pulling taffy."

Mrs Madison lowered her chin and gazed at her over a pair of imaginary glasses. "My son wanted to pull taffy."

"Yes. Saltwater taffy. And afterward he left and I rode home with my sister in the buggy."

"And that's what made your father tell you to quit?"

The accusation that she had been dancing around the truth still stung. No more dancing. Chance's mother wasn't going to leave until she got what she came for.

"There was a little more to it than that."

"Patty. I'm running out of both time and patience. Tell me exactly what happened." She didn't sound angry. She sounded halfway between angry and afraid, which couldn't be right. She doubted that Taylor Madison was afraid of anything, including blizzards and escaped bulls.

"Among the Amish," she said at last, "when a man takes a woman home, it means something. That he wants to court her. I know Chance couldn't have known that," she added hastily. "I said no, of course, but everyone who was there knows he asked. It—it might have given rise to talk—it did, actually, because someone told my father. So he stepped in to prevent its happening again."

Patricia felt like a balloon that had not burst, but simply lost all its air.

Mrs Madison gazed at her, waiting to see if she'd say anything else. "I see," she said after a minute. "Well, I can't change your father's mind, and I see that you're not about to, either. But I will speak to Chance and tell him what you've said. He's not happy about your leaving. He thinks it's his fault."

Goodness gracious, could this get any worse? "Oh, no, Mrs Madison. Please don't speak to him. Not about the—the courting. That would only embarrass him, and I'm already embarrassed enough for both of us."

"Yes, I see that. Very well. I'll just mention that what he did was frowned on in Amish culture and leave it at that."

"Thank you," Patricia said, hardly audible even to herself.

"Carry on, Patty," she said with an air of putting the whole conversation behind her. "You'll want to do Cabin Six next. We expect them right after lunch, and I know you have to go at noon."

So the schedule had said, but Patricia only nodded and gripped the handle of her cart. Mrs Madison held the door for her, and she pushed it out on to the manicured path that led between the cabins.

She let out a huge breath once she was out of sight. Now she knew how the deer felt when the hunters walked past and kept on going. She would never have expected Taylor Madison to ask her to stay on against her father's wishes. At least she hadn't offered to go and plead her case with Dat! Patricia would never have lived it down.

Honestly, *Englisch* young folk had it so much easier. No misunderstandings, no centuries-old customs that clashed so embarrassingly with modern ways. If she'd been on *Rumspringe*, would Dat have put his foot down like this? Would she have been able to keep her job?

It took two seconds for Patricia to go from toying with the idea of *Rumspringe* to deciding on it. She'd tell her parents tonight she was going to begin now. She'd say she intended to keep working at the Rocking Diamond, and that they shouldn't expect her to go to as many things with Clara. She'd have her own doings to go to. She wasn't quite sure yet what those would be, but she knew some of Julie Stolzfus's worldly hockey friends. She could ask what they were up to on Friday nights.

And if she wanted to accept a ride from Chance Madison, she would. Maybe he'd even ask her out on a proper date, to the ice cream shop, or to a movie. She'd never been to a movie. It was about time she did.

Rumspringe was all about freedom, wasn't it? Knowing enough about the other side of the fence to make up her mind which side she wanted to live on?

Well, up until now she'd never even considered the grass on the other side.

As of today, green was going to be her favorite color.

LIKE MOST OF THE BUSINESSES ALONG THE MAIN SHOPPING street in Mountain Home, Rose Garden Quilts stayed open late on Thursdays and Fridays. Patricia worked one to eight, with a break for dinner around four. So, according to Dat's edict, Clara waited for her with the buggy at the bottom of the Rocking Diamond's lane. It was about half a mile's walk from the house to the county highway, but it gave Patricia time to think out what she was going to say.

She climbed in and settled herself on the passenger's side. "Hallo."

"Hallo yourself." Clara shook the reins over the horse's back. "Only one more day of being your personal driver." She didn't sound angry, only factual.

Patricia decided that she'd practice her reasoning on her sister. "Don't be so sure. I've made up my mind to go on *Rumspringe* this summer—well, what's left of it. Or maybe longer." No law said she had to stop for roundup. That was simply one of the major events of the ranching year. Nothing to do with her personal life.

The reins went loose in Clara's hands, and the horse tossed its head as if to bring this to her attention. "You're joking." She tightened them and the horse resumed its pace.

"*Neh*. I'm not baptized, and you and the boys all had your chance. Why shouldn't I?"

"I didn't think you wanted one," Clara said. "I thought you'd start baptism classes after Christmas. A couple of the *Youngie* have already asked the bishop about it. I thought you'd be with them."

"Well, you thought wrong. I'm going to tell Mamm and Dat tonight. Don't you go blabbing, now. I want to tell them myself, when I get home."

"Who else knows?"

She was not going to admit that she'd already told Gideon Miller. Because that would mean something, and Clara would leap to a conclusion that simply wasn't true.

"I just made up my mind today. You're the first person I've spoken to about it."

"But—but a week ago it hadn't even entered your head. At least, not that I could see. What changed, *Schweschder*?"

"Taylor Madison spoke to me today. She wanted to know the real reason why I handed in my notice."

"Did you tell her it was her son?"

"I didn't want to, but she wouldn't leave me alone until I did. I hope he doesn't hate me for bringing his mother's wrath down on his head."

"Don't be so dramatic." As they passed the Circle M access road where the cattle trucks came to collect the animals going to market, Clara waved. Seth and Gideon were on horseback away in the distance, and one of them lifted his arm in greeting. "What does Taylor Madison have to do with *Rumspringe?*"

Patricia sighed. "Just that if I was, Dat wouldn't have much to say about where I worked or who I got rides with. He'd just have to put up with it. And I wouldn't have to quit."

"You don't want to?" She made a sound like *pshhhh.* "I don't know how you can work at a dude ranch. So many worldly people, all wanting things at once. I'd go crazy."

Clara was happiest at home, where things tended to be predictable day after day. And when they weren't, she was better equipped to deal with them from a position of familiarity. Patricia was the opposite. She liked every day to be different. And while her duties didn't change much in either of her workplaces, there were just enough *Englisch* folks walking in the door, all with interesting lives and needs, to keep her on her toes. She liked to help them get what they wanted, whether that meant fabric or directions to the best hiking trails up in the mountains.

"Well, I don't want to quit. You have to admit the money is *gut.* I don't want to give that up."

"I know you're saving." They were on the outskirts of town now. "But I thought it was for your hope chest."

"I don't have any hopes," Patricia quipped. "Or a chest."

"But I saw you dig a couple of old dresses out of the rag bag. Are you going to humor Aendi Annie and start a wedding quilt?"

"I'm ahead of you. I bought a couple of fat quarters the other day. And I've thought of a pattern."

"Aendi will be thrilled that you're listening to her. Keeping up a tradition that's nonsense. And maybe even sinful." Clara passed the quilt shop and turned into the yard of the feed store, which was the closest place to turn the buggy around if you weren't going to tie up the horse and go shopping.

"How is the story of the wedding quilt sinful?" It might be kind of silly and charming, but surely not that.

"It's putting your trust in an object and the traditions of men," Clara said. "Not in *Gott* bringing you together with the person He wants for you in His own *gut* time."

"I think you're taking it all too seriously. And I hope you haven't said that to Aendi. It would hurt her feelings."

Clara dropped her gaze to the reins in her hands. "Am I too judgmental?"

Patricia held her thumb and forefinger about a quarter inch apart. "Maybe just this much."

"I'm not making sense, am I?" Her sister's brows knit in a frown. "Getting worked up about a story and not about you going on *Rumspringe* at your age."

"Not as advanced as yours," Patricia fired back, and hopped down before Clara could zing her in return. "Thanks for the ride. See you at eight."

She cut through the feed store and resisted the urge to browse the seed and gardening aisle. At the end of it, instead of the display of big ceramic pots they'd had all week, there were a number of bicycles leaning against each other in all different colors.

The sight of them stopped her in her tracks. A bicycle!

If she had one, Clara wouldn't need to drive her around. She could go to work, to town, to the library ... to a movie, if she wanted to. No horse to pasture, no buggy to find room for. A bicycle fit anywhere—even in the back of a truck. And she was pretty sure that bicycles weren't forbidden by the *Ordnung*. They might not even be *in* the *Ordnung*. With Montana having three seasons that didn't lend themselves to cycling and only one short one that did, it might just have been overlooked here, since no one in the *Gmay* bothered with them.

A glance at the clock told her she had three minutes to get to work.

"Dottie?" she said to the owner's wife behind the counter. "How much is one of these bicycles?"

"They're used, but they're in good shape. Everett got them at an estate sale," Dottie said. "That one you've got your hand on, it's called a California Cruiser. Supposed to be good for your back, because you're not all hunched over. It's a three-speed, so not too fancy, either, like one of those mountain bikes that has eighteen gears like a diesel rig. He's asking forty dollars."

She had forty dollars. "Can you put it away for me? I can go to the bank and bring the money during my dinner break."

"Better climb on and see if it's the right size first."

Patricia hadn't known that bicycles came in sizes. But when Dottie pronounced it a perfect fit, she took it away into the back and Patricia had less than a minute to scoot out the door and jog down the boardwalk to the quilt shop.

A bicycle! Well, if that didn't convince Dat she meant what she said about *Rumspringe*, nothing would.

And the best part? It was a pretty robin's-egg color. If she squinted, she could even say it was green.

❦ 9 ❦

MOUNTAIN HOME

IT TOOK about an hour and a half to walk the five miles into Mountain Home, but Gideon got lucky before he set out around four o'clock. He'd expected Alden Stolzfus to spend the evening at the Circle M, but some iron stock he'd been waiting for had been delivered to the feed store, and he wanted to get it into his own shop before they closed.

Once in town, Gideon hopped out with a cheery, "*Denki*, future cousin-in-law," and, with a broad smile, Alden shook the reins over the horse's back and headed down the street.

Gideon wasn't sure what he expected, or even what he would say when he pushed open the door to Rose Garden Quilts. But the first thing he noticed was that Patricia King wasn't there.

"*Guder owed*, Gideon," Rose said, in the midst of pinning a pattern on the end of a rack of fabric that presumably went with it. "Was that Alden who dropped you off? I wasn't expecting him home—Julie and Beth are just making pizza for supper."

"I'm sure he'll be happy with that. Some stock came in, so

he hustled into town to get it before Everett closes. Is Patricia around?"

"*Ja*, she's on her dinner break. She said she had to go to the feed store, too. Probably not for iron stock, though."

He smiled, then wondered what business Patricia had at the feed store. Chicken feed, maybe? "I'll look in over there in case she needs some help."

"Get her to eat while you're at it. Usually she brings a sack lunch, but she didn't have anything with her today."

Getting Patricia King to do anything she didn't want to do was like hauling a calf out of a mudhole, but he didn't say that. He just nodded and ducked out the door.

From the clanking sounds out in the feed store's yard, Alden was collecting his stock. Gideon would go help him in a minute, but first he'd see if Patricia needed a hand. He followed the sound of feminine voices to the back room, where he found her in proud possession of ... a *bicycle*?

"Hi, Gideon." She wheeled it past him as though this was perfectly normal. "Look what I just bought. Isn't it great?"

"You bought that?"

"Yes, and if I knew where Clara was, I'd tell her not to bother picking me up later. I want to ride it home."

Would it even fit in a buggy? "Does it have lights on it?"

"Of course it does," Dottie the owner's wife said, following them into the store. "I showed Patricia where the switch is. It's not very bright, so it will need a new battery soon, but it ought to get her home, anyway."

"It even has a basket." Patricia plunked her little backpack into it, her entire being radiating satisfaction.

He had about a hundred more questions, but she wheeled the bike out the back door into the yard and climbed on, taking a few practice circles around Alden and the pile of iron bars.

"Gideon, just the man I need," Alden said when he spotted him in the doorway. "Give us a hand loading this into the wagon?"

The farrier's wagon was bigger, more the size of a family buggy, and the entire load of stock fit in it.

"Sure Timothy can pull it?" Everett pushed his MOUNTAIN HOME FEED & SEED cap up to scratch his sweating forehead.

"I'm sure. *Denki*, Gideon," he said in *Deitsch*. "I'm all right from here."

Timothy, his big Belgian, leaned into the traces and cautiously, he and Alden trundled to the yard entrance and crossed the highway to the blacksmith shop.

Meanwhile, Patricia looked as though she was going to take off at twice the pace of the big horse, once it was out of the yard.

"Patricia, wait!" Was it his imagination, or was that unwillingness he saw in her posture as she brought the bike to a halt? "Rose said you forgot your dinner. Maybe we could grab a sandwich at the Dutch Café?"

She gazed at him from the bike, one foot on the ground, the other on a pedal. "And have Susan spread a rumor that you took me there on a date?"

"At four-thirty in the afternoon?"

"I don't think she's particular about details when it comes to a *gut* piece of gossip."

She made it sound juicy, like they would have been up to something. And what was wrong with being seen with him on a date? Not that she had anything to worry about, but still—he wasn't *that* bad a prospect.

"Okay, then, how about the Duck Blind? Their burgers are

pretty good." It was one of those food trucks, and parked pretty much anywhere it wanted, because the two guys who did the cooking knew their way around a burger and tended to bring in a nice crowd of customers. When she didn't reply, he said, "Come on, I'm hungry. And you only have half an hour for dinner, *nix?*"

Finally she nodded. "All right. I saw the truck at the gas station. I'll meet you there."

Before he could even reply, she was off, her skirts flapping as she pedaled off down the road, *Kapp* strings blowing out behind her. And then the *Kapp* lifted from the front in the wind of her going—she reached up to grab it with one hand— and it blew off entirely, tumbling through the air like a white cotton kite.

Gideon was already running. The *Kapp* landed twenty yards behind her in the westbound lane. A van was coming around the curve, but he could make it. He ran across the highway, snatched up the *Kapp* in mid-stride, and amid the strident blaring of the van's horn, reached the sidewalk.

When he caught up to her, her eyes were huge. "You could have been killed!" She took her *Kapp* and brushed at it, and with her head bowed, he got a full view of her shiny brown hair, neatly wound from the front in two waves that tucked into her *bob*, the coiled bun at the back of her head. She slipped the *Kapp* on and settled it, then tied the strings not on her chest, the way many girls did, but under her chin. "*Denki*, Gideon. That van would have smashed it flat."

"I'm glad it didn't smash *me* flat. That was a close shave."

She walked the bike now instead of riding it, beside him on the sidewalk. "Since I'm spending money today, let me buy your hamburger as a thank-you."

He shook his head, imagining what his brother Tobias

would say if he heard that Gideon had taken advantage of her in such a way. "If you like, we'll each buy our own. That way we'll have receipts to prove it wasn't a date."

She laughed. "I don't think the Duck Blind gives receipts."

"Then we'll ask them to write out testimonials. *Gideon Miller and Patricia King just happened to arrive at the same time and order burgers separately. Signed, the proprietors.*"

"All right, all right, I take back what I said about the date."

At the gas station, where fortunately the Duck Blind was still parked with a short line of customers, there was nowhere to put the bike but to lean it on the fence. She ordered some fancy burger with Brie cheese and mushrooms, and he ordered a cheeseburger whose only claim to fanciness was dill pickles. They split an order of fries, but since there was nowhere to set it down, they used the basket of the bicycle.

Gideon was happy not to talk until he took the edge off his hunger with half the burger. When Patricia slowed down a little, too, and started on the fries, she said, "Have you mentioned to anyone that I was thinking about *Rumspringe?*"

His mouth full, he could only say, "Noah."

She narrowed her eyes at him. "So he could talk me out of it?"

"I think he knows better." There, that was a good non-answer.

"Mind you," she went on, "I told Clara on the way into town today, and she's probably already blabbed to Dat. I wanted to tell him and Mamm myself."

Gideon swallowed mightily. "Might be better for them to have the afternoon to cool off."

"Maybe. I'm still going to tell them. I don't plan to quit the Rocking Diamond, after all."

About to take the next bite, he paused. "You don't? But I thought your father said no."

"If I'm on *Rumspringe*, and I'm not baptized, there's no reason I can't keep working there. Mrs Madison wants me to stay on."

"Mrs Madison isn't what worries your dad." He took the bite to prevent himself from saying any more.

"She's going to speak to Chance." She rolled her eyes. "I'm sure that will go over well. He'll be so embarrassed he'll never speak to me again."

"Which is sort of the point, *nix*?"

Having just stuffed in a bunch of fries, all she could do was glare. When she could speak, she said, "I'm not a child. Neither is he. I know what's appropriate and what's not. And unlike *some* people, I can see a lonely man behind the *Englisch* clothes and the giant pickup."

"He can't be that lonely. There are nothing but people all over that ranch. Plus his two brothers."

"Two brothers he doesn't get along with."

"And you know this how?"

She popped the last bite of the burger into her mouth and chomped it like she was punishing it. "I work there, Gideon. I see them, I hear them, I stay out of their way. Honestly, I don't know why Mr Madison doesn't do anything about those two. A day's work cleaning out horse stalls would work wonders."

"He probably can't make them. I don't think anyone has said no to those boys since they were born."

"Anyway, I'll deal with them."

"How? You weigh a hundred and twenty soaking wet. How are you going to deal with a pair of bullies like Trey and Clint?"

"I'm not. Zefra will. Or their mother will."

"I sure hope so. Honest, Patricia, even if your dad hadn't

said a thing, I'd think twice about going back there. You're the only Amish girl on the place, and Zefra and Mrs Madison can't be with you every second."

"I hope not. None of us would get anything done." Her eyebrows crinkled into a frown. "I have thought twice. I'm not giving up my job. And while I appreciate your concern, I don't need advice from someone who's never worked there and doesn't know the situation."

She might as well have planted both palms on his chest and pushed him away. "Fine," he said shortly. "I was just trying to help."

"No, you were just trying to tighten the reins my father already put on me." She tilted her chin. "I have to get back to work." After wiping her hands on a napkin, she took all the trash to the can at the end of the food truck, dumping it all in as though she was tossing out the conversation right along with it. Then she got on the bike.

"Patricia, wait!" He put out a hand, but she wheeled out of reach. "What about Friday?"

"I have to work until eight," she called over her shoulder. "If you want to be the boss of someone, try Susanna."

And she pedaled off across the highway and back to the quilt shop, leaving him with a five-mile walk and the feeling that, if he'd been trying to be her friend, he'd have been better off staying on the Circle M.

At least there the dog listened to him.

FOR THE REST OF THE EVENING, IN THE QUIET MOMENTS when there were no customers in the shop, Patricia fumed about Gideon. What right did he have to act like her elder brother? Or worse, her father? Honestly, had his sister taught him nothing about how to act with young women?

She was well aware he was behaving like a *Bruder* and looking out for her. But it didn't feel that way. Here she was, looking forward to freedom, when every word he said seemed to wrap around her like a constraint.

When Clara arrived with the buggy, things didn't improve. Since it was such a nice evening, she'd driven the open two-seater that people called a courting buggy, even though everyone knew a courting couple had far more privacy in a closed one.

Clara's eyes practically fell out of her head. Patricia had locked up the shop, gone out the back, and ridden the bicycle up next to her on the boardwalk. "What are you doing with that?" she said, as aghast as if Patricia had plunked down her entire life savings on a car.

"Riding it home, obviously, since you didn't bring the other buggy."

"Patricia, you can't—"

Oh, but she could. She tied her *Kapp* strings firmly under her chin—Aendi Annie would be so happy to see that, since it signified submission. Sadly for her great-aunt, she only did it so her *Kapp* wouldn't go flying off again into the road.

Before Clara could get the buggy turned around, Patricia had already pedaled past the gas station, where the Duck Blind was closing up for the night, the wind in her face smelling like hay and dust. But it didn't take long for Clara to catch up, and she stuck to her like a burr, as though lending her protection from behind.

When they finally reached home, Patricia was breathless and her legs ached. Clearly a person had to work up to this, not pedal five miles west and one north on her very first ride.

Mamm and Dat were enjoying the evening on the front porch with Aendi Annie, but the conversation stopped abruptly as the little parade she and Clara made came to a halt.

"Patricia, what on earth—" Mamm practically squeaked.

"I drove all the way to town for nothing," Clara groused, urging the horse into motion and heading for the barn. "I'll wait for your *denkes*," she said to Patricia over her shoulder.

She'd have to make it up to her sister, whose surprise seemed to have been engulfed by annoyance over those six miles. But right now Patricia had bigger fish to fry.

"Isn't it pretty?" she said brightly, dismounting and leaning the bicycle on one of the farmhouse's porch posts. "They had it at the feed store for only forty dollars."

"And what ... is the purpose ...?" Dat seemed to be having trouble speaking.

"Now Clara doesn't have to drive me everywhere. I got home in almost the same time as she could drive." She rushed on. "I can go to the Rocking Diamond, into town, to any doings of the *Youngie* I want to go to ... now that I'm starting my *Rumspringe*." With a smile that she hoped didn't tremble with the butterflies in her stomach, she seated herself on the top step, arranged her skirts, and wrapped her hands around one knee.

"I see why you had to tie on your covering," Aendi Annie observed in the silence.

Nobody reacted to the R-word. It was almost like they hadn't heard it. Or didn't want to.

"*Ja*, it flew off in town," Patricia admitted. "Luckily Gi— one of the boys caught it before a van ran over it. I learned that lesson pretty quick." She untied the strings and let them dangle down the front as usual.

"Here's another lesson for you," her father said. "Tomorrow

you can take that bicycle back to where you got it, and ask for a refund."

Perhaps it hadn't been the best idea to bring in the harvest before she'd prepared the ground a little.

"But I'll need transportation while I'm running around," she said, hoeing in. "We can't spare a buggy, and if I'm doing things like going to work at the Rocking Diamond, or going out with friends, I can't walk everywhere, or expect people to pick me up."

"You spent forty dollars on a bicycle you're only going to use for one day?" Mamm asked, clearly in connection with the Rocking Diamond.

"I'm not quitting my job there, Mamm," she said as gently and reasonably as she could. "Mrs Madison spoke to me today, and asked me to stay on."

"And I asked you to stay away," Dat said.

"Because of Chance," she said, nodding as if she agreed. "But his mother is going to speak to him, so there shouldn't be anything to worry about now."

"Not if he's as disobedient as you are."

"I'm sorry you think so, Dat," Patricia said soberly. "But the custom here says I can take some time to run around before I make the serious decision on whether or not to join church. The boys and Clara had that opportunity. I know I'm a little older than they were, but I want it, too."

She had him there, and he knew it, from the way his lips clamped shut.

"You may be entitled to take that time if you wish," Mamm said, "but you're not entitled to disobey your father when he has expressly forbidden you to work at that dude ranch."

"Andrew disobeyed you both when he went to work at the ski hill," she said bravely, the butterflies swooping in her stomach. "And even Simeon worked for that *Englisch* outfit, building RVs, when you didn't want him to."

"He was seventeen," Dat managed past his tight lips.

"And I'm twenty-one, and not likely to be drawn into a life of sin and dissipation." She tried to smile, as if she were making a joke.

"You won't be living here if you are."

This was not the direction she wanted the conversation to go. "But a *gut* job, and a bit of fun, whether it's in town or with the *Youngie* ... there's nothing wrong with that. Nothing wrong with trying out the grass on the other side of the fence."

"You might find a stinging nettle or two," Aendi Annie said quietly, gazing over the fields her husband and sons had once worked, and that Dat now had in hay, the acres in alfalfa leased to the Petersheims.

"I might," Patricia agreed. "And it will serve me right if I grab one without thinking first. But that's part of it, isn't it?"

"I don't like it," Dat said. "You're not like Clara. You're as stubborn as Sim, and I don't want to think about Andrew and what he put us through."

"I won't do anything like that, Dat." And she meant it. Andrew had put his share of grey into their mother's brown hair. "I just want to spread my wings a little. Not fly away completely."

Her father stood and held out a hand to Aendi Annie. "Time to call it a day," he said to her. "I'll see you over to the *Daadi Haus*, Aendi."

Annie tucked her hand into the crook of his elbow and let him act as her support across the lawn to the little house where she lived.

Mamm didn't speak as she went inside. In a moment, the window glowed with the golden light of a lantern.

"I guess that subject is closed," Patricia said to no one in particular.

There hadn't exactly been enthusiastic agreement. But they hadn't forbidden it, either.

Well, Patricia could work with that. To prove how cooperative she was, she wheeled her pretty bicycle into the barn so none of her family would have to look at it.

10

THE WILD ROSE AMISH INN

Friday, August 12

IF PATRICIA HAD WANTED to cause a sensation when she arrived at the volleyball game after work Friday night, she got her wish in spades. They could see her coming, of course—the Wild Rose Amish Inn was only five minutes' walk from Rose Garden Quilts, and the sky was still warm with the gloaming as she crossed the highway with a cheery wave. Dave Yoder, who was serving the volleyball, gawked and missed his serve, to the derision of the others, and by the time she pedaled into the parking lot and leaned the bike against the garden fence, half the *Youngie* had jogged up the slope to get a good look.

"Where did you get this?"

"Your parents really allowed it?"

"Never mind her parents—what is the bishop going to say?"

Laughing, she told them about the other bikes at the feed store, and the words were barely out of her mouth when Calvin Yoder, Orin Petersheim, and Julie Stolzfus took off at a gallop down the slope, through the woods to the variety store's parking lot, and across the highway to the feed store.

"Now you've done it," Susanna Miller said at her shoulder. "They don't close until nine—just watch all three of them come back on bicycles."

And sure enough, they did. Calvin's monstrosity had studded tires and was painted black, as though it could take on the steepest mountain path. Julie's was fast and sleek, just like her. And Orin had chosen a very plain one that didn't even have gears, but he seemed really happy to have it.

Well, it wasn't her fault if others among the *Youngie* needed a practical form of transportation. And two of these three were even baptized. Honestly, why had no one thought of riding bikes before?

"You've started a fashion." Clara joined her as she walked across the lawn toward the scent of food.

On the patio, Gideon and Seth were barbecuing hot dogs, and on the grass beyond, Luke and Rachel had set up a cooking table, where three big pots cooled on single propane burners, releasing the sweetness of just-boiled taffy into the air. Sarah Jane presided over them, with Cathy Petersheim and one of the *Englisch* guests helping to pour the mixture into bread pans that would form the loaves of taffy to be pulled.

She and Clara lined up with the others. "Not much of a fashion," she told her over her shoulder. "They only had half a dozen."

Dave Yoder, ahead of her, managed to overhear. "If the bishop approves, Dat can order bicycles into the store. But not until he approves."

"Why wouldn't he?" Patricia said. "Lots of communities have them."

"Not back in Kentucky," Clara reminded her. To Dave, she

said, "The *Ordnung* only allows push scooters where we grew up."

"Look at Pinecraft," Patricia said on a burst of inspiration. "I've never been there, but I've seen pictures. Men and women of all ages pedaling around on contraptions that are a cross between a shopping cart and a tricycle."

"Pinecraft and Kentucky aren't the Siksika Valley," Dave said, clearly feeling the need to emphasize the obvious. "If Little Joe, the deacons, and the preacher don't agree on bicycles, there won't be bicycles."

"There will be for me," she said, his tone rubbing her the wrong way. "As of today, I'm on *Rumspringe*."

Dave turned to stare at her, though he was almost at the front of the line. "At your age? What on earth for?"

Why did people insist on saying *At your age?* as if she were fifty?

"What do you want on your hot dog, Dave?" Seth asked, and she was saved from a reply by David's having to choose chopped onions, chili, shredded cheese, lettuce and tomato, or all of the above.

When it was her turn, she picked chili and cheese, and moved down the table to get a wedge of watermelon. Rachel invited the *Englisch* folks to join the line, and Luke took off his canvas apron to enjoy the fruit of his labors, too.

"I love this place," Patricia heard a woman in cutoff shorts sigh to the one who had been helping with the taffy. "We found it on the Internet, and I swear I've gained five pounds since Wednesday."

"There's taffy yet to come," her companion said. "It's like living in *Anne of Green Gables*—only with hot dogs and a barbecue."

Patricia had read several of Lucy Maud Montgomery's books, including the one whose heroine shared a name with her. She hadn't liked *Pat of Silver Bush* much—she preferred Anne, always having the best intentions yet always getting into scrapes.

And always being forgiven.

They sat on the grass, leaving the Adirondack chairs on the wraparound porch for Rachel's guests. The grass was cool and smelled *gut*, and nobody cared if you spilled anything in it. Especially since Calvin and David decided to join her and Clara, with Julie and Orin doing the same. Luckily, Dave and his gloomy-gus attitude got drowned out by the happy chatter of the others, telling her all about how they'd chosen their bicycles.

"First thing I'm going to do is see how long it takes me to get out to the state park," Calvin said around his second hot dog. "And then I'm going to ride some trails."

"You'd better see if you can do some deliveries for Dat while you're at it," Dave got in. "Put that bike to work instead of play."

"I can do both," Calvin said. "That's a *gut* idea, *Bruder*."

"Better not make too many plans until we see what the bishop says," Dave said for the second time. "I hope the feed store has a thirty-day return policy."

"Who's going to ask him?" Calvin wanted to know, looking around at their little group.

"Patricia started it," Dave said a little smugly. "Maybe she should."

That rascal. Was he getting back at her for mentioning Pinecraft? Or simply for being the first to do something interesting? Dave was such a stick in the mud. He was as traditional as Dat, and that was saying something. No wonder he couldn't get a girl to date him more than three times. Nobody wanted to marry their father.

"I'm sure when he hears about it, he'll let Julie and Calvin know," she said airily. "Orin and I aren't baptized yet, so I doubt he'll concern himself with us."

That seemed to keep Dave quiet, thank goodness. And even though Orin was only nineteen, he shyly asked if he could be her partner to pull taffy.

"That would be fun," she said with a big smile as Gideon and Seth Miller walked past with their plates, finally having served the whole line. "I hope Sarah Jane and Cathy mixed up the kind with the sprinkles in it. If we get some of that, all I ask is that you don't drop it in the grass."

Orin's mouth twisted ruefully. "I wasn't there last week, but I heard that Madison kid spoiled yours. I'll try to do better."

"Accidents happen," Clara put in, with a sidelong glance at Calvin. "The point is to have wrapped candy of all different flavors to take home. That loaf wasn't my sister's personal property."

"We should make sure Rachel gets a big bowl of it for her guests," Patricia suggested. "It was kind of her to let us have our frolic here."

"I think the guests are enjoying it," Julie said. "Chance Madison should have come to this one. He'd have fit in better."

That was the first time anyone had shown any sympathy for the young *Englisch* man. Patricia smiled at her in appreciation.

"Hey, isn't that him?" Julie looked past Patricia to the highway, where Chance's big red truck slowed to make the left turn into Creekside Lane. "He can't be coming here, can he?"

A moment later the gravel in the parking lot crunched under a set of tires, and the bass rumble of the engine shut off.

"I can't believe this," Dave muttered. "Next time you want to prophesy, Julie, resist the urge."

She ignored him, wordlessly taking Patricia's empty plate and getting up as Chance ambled across the grass toward them.

Toward her.

Patricia rose, too, brushing grass and crumbs off her dress and meeting him near the fence where her bike was leaning with the others. "Hallo, Chance. What are you doing here?"

He shoved his hands in his pockets and rocked back on the heels of his cowboy boots. "I saw you all on the lawn and wondered if it was another gig like last Friday." He nodded toward the volleyball nets down by the barn. "I guess so."

It was one thing for her to invite him one time. Why he'd decided to invite himself tonight was beyond her. Lonely or not, she sure hoped he didn't plan to make a habit of it. But they were at the Inn, and Rachel Miller's hospitality demanded kindness.

Or it would, if Gideon and Seth Miller weren't striding across the grass like they meant business.

"The hot dogs should still be warm," she said with a smile. "Chili dogs with the works, and watermelon if you want it."

"Why, thanks," he said. "I didn't get dinner. I was—"

"Chance," Gideon greeted him with the kind of smile people put on when they wanted to sell you something. "Didn't expect to see you here at my mother's place."

"I was just telling Patricia I saw you all from the road, and thought if those big pots meant taffy, I could try my luck again, and do better this time."

Patricia could see Gideon's quandary. Honestly, he should

simply have minded his own business and not made such a show of marching over here. Because either he backed down and Chance joined them, or he told him to go away. And that second option would not be very wise.

Well, she was the only person here that Chance knew as a friend. It was up to her to do something.

"Practice makes perfect," she said to him with a smile. "Go and grab a hot dog. They poured the taffy before supper, so it should be almost ready to pull."

"I promise I won't drop ours this time," he said.

Ours? From the corner of her eye, she saw Gideon bristle like a barn cat's tail. "Oh, I already have a partner to pull with. But there are plenty of other people here."

"A couple of the guests want to give it a try," Seth said to him. "Since you've got experience, they'd probably appreciate learning what to do."

Chance actually smiled at the prospect, and headed off toward the barbecue, where foil-covered trays held the hot dogs and trimmings.

"Nice save, Seth," she remarked, using Julie's hockey vernacular. Then she rounded on Gideon. "What were *you* going to say to him?"

He backed away a step in surprise. "Nothing. This is my mother's place. I just came to find out why he was here, bothering us all again."

"He wasn't bothering anyone. Maybe he wants a friend," she hissed.

"I bet he does. He headed straight for you. And don't tell me you're the only person he knows. He's talked to Seth and me a hundred times at work."

She rolled her eyes in exasperation. "Gideon Miller, use your head. If word gets back to the Madisons that you made him feel unwelcome, or worse, if you tell him to leave, do you have any idea of the harm they could do to your mother's business?"

He stared at her, and she realized that no, he hadn't even thought of that.

She resisted the urge to throw up her hands. "Someone should tell Rachel that he's willing to show any of her guests who wants to learn what to do."

"Better he has an *Englisch* partner than one of our *Maedscher*," Seth murmured. "I'll go, and Mamm can introduce him as one of the local ranchers."

"And if there's any Amish girl you don't want partnering with him, better ask her quick." Patricia couldn't resist adding. Talk about overprotective!

"Who's your partner?"

"Orin," she said airily. "We both have bikes now."

"So do I," Calvin put in, getting up with his plate. "Clara, do you want to pull with me?"

"If it keeps you far away from the cooking pots," she replied.

Patricia hadn't realized her sister was so brave. Or so crazy. She was one of the few girls left in the valley who hadn't been asked out by Calvin Yoder. Goodness knew what disasters this act of charity could lead to.

The taffy wasn't quite cool enough to handle, so Patricia made herself scarce in the Inn's kitchen with Susanna and Cathy Petersheim who, she suspected, was also staying out of Calvin's way. For the number of people in the yard, the dishes went surprisingly fast. Mind you, Rachel had run out of ordinary plates and had to use paper ones for most of the *Youngie*, so that made less to clean up.

She hung up her dish towel and then she and Cathy looked

at one another. "Who are you pulling with?" Patricia asked in a low voice, since there were guests right in the next room. "You're safe from Calvin—my sister is his partner."

If anyone could handle Calvin, it was Clara. She was so literal and practical that Calvin wouldn't get an inch of leeway. And with enough good sense for both of them, she might even keep him from embarrassing himself.

Cathy heaved a breath of relief. "Thanks for telling me. I was prepared to spend the whole evening in here, but I'm glad I don't have to. Rachel wants everyone to enjoy it, so I think I'll ask one of these nice *Englisch* women to pull with me. That will keep me well out of his way."

Patricia went outside and found Orin, and to her delight, their first pull was the vanilla one with the sprinkles. They found themselves ranged with several other pairs in a row on the lawn, a safe distance from the cooking pots, with Chance and a middle-aged lady on one side of them pulling strawberry, and on the other, Cathy and a younger one who looked like the lady's daughter pulling what smelled like lime. The electric fairy lights strung along the porch roof that Luke had connected to a tiny generator helped the lanterns throw enough light. At least twenty pairs of Amish *Youngie* and *Englisch* tourists laughed and yelped as they got wound up in taffy, extricated themselves, and tried not to eat too many of the escaped pieces.

As they finished pulling and wound a rope of taffy to cut, Orin murmured, "Hope you don't think I'm running out on you, but I want to ask my sister something before B—before people start heading home."

Patricia did her best not to smile and say, *Such as whether her friend Beth Keim might let you drive her home from church next week?* "You go right ahead. It only takes one person to cut and wrap anyway."

Orin slipped away into the dark, and Gideon Miller took his place. "It goes faster with two." His capable fingers wrapped a piece of waiting taffy, twisted both ends efficiently, and tossed it in the bowl in the middle of the table.

Wordlessly, she picked up the knife and began to slice one-inch pieces off the sweet-smelling roll. "Are you and your partner finished?"

"I didn't have a partner. I've been helping Luke with the barbecue and the propane burners, and putting food away. Seth and Chance are practically holding a taffy class for a bunch of *Englisch* kids who just came home. That's what all the *Gedunner* is over there."

Home. He lived and worked at the Circle M, but she supposed that this was home—where his family was.

"I saw your sister pulling with Calvin. Wouldn't have expected that."

"I hope they're having fun."

"It's hard to tell, with Clara. But Calvin was."

Now it was her turn to bristle. "What do you mean, it's hard to tell?"

He held up a piece of taffy like a white flag. "I just meant she's a serious person. Not like you."

If he thought this was making it better, he could think again. "Are you quite done with your criticism, Gideon Miller? Because if so, you're quite welcome to find someone else to *help*."

"I want to help you."

"Lucky me."

"Because if I'm working with you on the taffy, then Chance

Madison won't be. And I wasn't criticizing either you or Clara. She is a serious person. You're more ... lively."

Crickets were lively. Trout were lively. As compliments went, this was distinctly lacking.

"So you're only here to keep Chance away. And here I thought it was for the pleasure of my company."

"Your company is like my mother's Hatch chile salsa. Painful in some ways, but a person can't help coming back for more." He grinned, as though his own humor tickled him.

Patricia did not snap. She did not lose her temper. She simply handed the knife to Clara, who chose that moment to appear with Calvin and a neat rope of blue bubblegum taffy. Then she walked away without another word, leaving the three of them staring after her.

11

"WHAT DID YOU SAY TO HER?" Clara King asked Gideon after a moment. She coiled the blue rope of glossy taffy on the cutting board and began to cut the free end into neat pieces. Without being asked, Calvin picked up a square of waxed paper and joined Gideon in his labors.

"Nothing," Gideon said, sounding as perplexed as he felt. "I gave her a compliment and she just … walked off."

"Some compliment," Calvin said. "Did you tell her she smelled like liniment? I heard one of the hands say that to my sister once. He liked this particular kind. But when he came into the variety store the next time, she made sure she wasn't around to help him."

"Neh." Gideon frowned at the wrapped candy between his fingers and tossed it in the bowl. "I can't figure her out."

"Does she need to be figured out?" Clara asked, glancing up at him. "Can't she just be accepted?"

How could you accept something you couldn't understand? That might work for Chinook arches and *Englisch* cars, but with women, a man needed something more.

"She thinks I criticize her."

"Do you?" Calvin's eyebrows went up as he made a scared face. "That's no way to get a date with a girl."

This from the man who made girls run away on sight. "I don't want a date with her!" When people glanced down the table at him, he lowered his voice, his cheeks burning. "I'd just like a normal conversation. I've been trying to talk with her about Chance Madison, but she just gets mad. And now with her going on *Rumspringe*, of all things, I'm downright worried."

"Don't be stepping into our father's shoes," Clara said, already having reduced the length of the blue coil by half. "That's not your place. Mind you, she stood up to him about working at the dude ranch. I think she's going back on Monday like nothing happened."

Gideon's stomach did a barrel roll. He'd been counting on her putting a little distance between herself and that family, willingly or not. "That's not *gut*."

"Why not?" Clara asked. "It's just a job."

Not to him, it wasn't. More like a rabbit in a field full of coyotes. "I've been working next door to those guys for six months, and nothing I've seen tells me an Amish woman should be around them." He paused. "Except maybe my Aendi Naomi. They walk pretty circumspectly around her."

"Only because Reuben is the best shot in the valley," Calvin joked.

"Ha ha." Gideon wondered if Calvin even knew that an Amish man was supposed to be gentle as a dove while he was being a pillar of strength for his family. He definitely wouldn't be waving firearms at people. If he did, he'd be asked to offer an apology in church, if he didn't get arrested by the *Englisch* police.

"Give her some space, Gideon." Clara cut the last piece of

taffy, put down the knife, and moved to the other side of the table so that the next pair could cut their taffy rope. While her clever fingers wrapped taffy, she said, "Do you want me to ask her why she's mad at you?"

He sighed. That would irritate Patricia even more. "*Denki*, but *neh*. I'll just mind my own business, I guess." It was fully dark now. "Time to hunt up a ride to the Circle M."

"Zach and Ruby are here," Calvin said. "You could probably go back with them."

Stuck in the back while an engaged couple made calf eyes at each other? Not likely. "Seth has probably found us a seat. I'll check with him."

Mamm had found colorful little paper bags for people to take their candy home in, so after making sure the big bowl in the dining room of the Inn was full, he filled a bag for his aunt and uncle. Reuben had a sweet tooth, and while there were umpteen ways to satisfy it in his own kitchen, saltwater taffy was a treat, for sure and certain.

Gideon circled the Inn, looking for Seth, but he wasn't around the house, or even inside. Maybe he was over by all the buggies, sweet-talking one of the *Youngie* from the west district into giving them a ride. That was the one thing about being a hand at the Circle M. Much as he liked working for Onkel Reuben, and loved the ranch itself, with the river and the orchard and the sheer beauty of the mountain peaks, not having his own buggy could sometimes put a stick in the wheel of a man's social life. There were three four-seaters at the ranch, but there were also more of his cousins than there were buggies. He could go to the frolics in a spring wagon, he supposed, but if he wanted to take a girl home, it had its limitations.

Clearly, when he got his pay after roundup, he was going to

have to write a letter to the buggy-maker in Colorado and put in an order.

He walked down the row of buggies, the moon and the lanterns hanging on one or two giving him enough light to see that, while a few of the young men were getting ready to go, Seth wasn't among them and they were from this end of the valley. He'd rather walk the five miles himself than ask someone to make a ten-mile round trip just for him.

Seth wasn't in the barn, or even up in the bunkhouse, which wasn't rented out yet, though it would be soon when the circuit hands rolled in to help with roundup. However, he could hear a pair of girls giggling and whispering in one of the rooms, so he beat a hasty retreat.

Where on earth was his brother? Maybe Mamm or Susanna knew.

He headed up the slope past the garden and saw that all of the bicycles that had been leaning on the deer fence were gone. It didn't take long to figure out—Calvin lived next door, behind the variety store, and Julie about two minutes away across the bridge. Orin lived a little farther out, past the schoolhouse, but still, not far.

And Patricia? She lived in the west district and had as far to go as he did. Had she really taken off, riding alone down the county highway? Or had she found a ride in a buggy big enough to accommodate the bicycle?

If he was perplexed before, he was downright worried now.

The growl of a big diesel engine penetrated the storm in his brain and cleared it like a lightning strike. Chance. With his big pickup. Who lived five minutes from the King place at a truck's speed.

Gideon took off across the grass and made it into the parking lot before Chance had even backed the pickup around.

He got a quick look inside the bed as he approached the driver's side window. No bicycle.

The window slid down silently. "Need a ride?"

"Thanks. But I can't ditch my brother. Not that I can find him—I've been looking all over."

"He left with Zach and that girl he's going to marry. The skinny one who doesn't talk."

Seth had ditched him? Nice. "That's Ruby, and they talk nonstop. Well, if he's gone, then I don't need to worry. The offer still good?"

"Yep. Got your taffy?"

He held up the bag as he circled the rumbling front of the truck. Then he climbed in and did up the seatbelt. "Did you have fun?" he said, because just listening to the engine was disconcerting, and he didn't want Chance to turn on the radio.

Chance crossed the Inn's little bridge over the rushing creek, turned right, and coasted through the stop sign at the highway. Then he accelerated through town as though the 35 MPH speed limit were merely a suggestion.

"Yeah, I did. Good, clean, wholesome fun."

Gideon couldn't tell whether he was being sarcastic or not. "Well, we Amish specialize in that. You did a good job with my mother's guests. They were pretty pleased at what they made, from what I could see."

After a moment, Chance said in a low tone, "I never taught someone something before."

"Not even your little brother?"

He shook his head. "Dad knows everything—or thinks he does. He showed us some stuff. Mom taught us to rope and ride. Clint mostly follows Trey around bugging him if he wants to learn something."

Gideon couldn't imagine not being taught by his father or

his older brother. And in turn teaching Seth the things he knew when he was old enough to get his foot into a stirrup or lift a rifle on a hunting trip.

"Well, I'm glad you got the chance tonight. Can you slow down some?"

"I could, but I gotta catch up to Patty. That light on her bike is useless. It's not safe on the highway unless you're lit up like the rodeo grounds on opening night."

"Patricia *rode home*?" What was the matter with that girl? Gideon didn't know whether to be more annoyed that Chance knew where Patricia was, or glad that this behemoth of a pickup would close the distance between them in record time.

"Yep. I didn't see her go, or I'd have given her a ride."

"Well, when we find her, we'll toss the bike in the back and do just that."

"That's the plan."

Okay, so now he sounded like Mr Obvious, but Gideon didn't care. Finding Patricia before an eighteen-wheeler did was the priority.

PATRICIA HADN'T PEDALED MORE THAN HALF A MILE PAST the town limits when she had to admit that she probably shouldn't have done this in the dark. But it was too late now. She couldn't exactly pedal back to the Inn and find someone who could take both her and the bike home. Everyone had probably gone.

Every time a car passed her, she flinched, convinced that it would sideswipe her and send her into the ditch with more than just a broken headlight. Could people not see her? The lady at the feed store had said the lights on the bike were in good working order, so why were the cars coming so close before they swerved to avoid her? She was riding on the wide shoulder, which was designed for buggies, but still.

She was nearly at the three-mile mark when she realized there was a pair of big, bright headlights coming up behind her —so bright she could see her own shadow thrown onto the asphalt in front. For just a moment, she wondered if she ought to pull off to the side until it passed. If it was an eighteen-wheeler, it might blow her right off the highway.

But the truck or diesel rig or whatever it was didn't seem inclined to pass. In fact, it seemed to be pacing her from a short distance back. For goodness sake, her hands were illuminated now. It was getting closer, but not passing. This couldn't be good.

A shiver of anxiety snaked through her stomach, and she picked up her pace, wishing the bike had more than three gears. Hadn't she seen a situation like this on one of the movie posters at the theater? A woman alone, backlit by the headlights of a truck. And she was pretty sure that movie had *not* been a romance.

Maybe there was a cattle gate she could duck through and head across the fields to safety. Maybe she should stop and demand to know what they thought they were doing. But no, that would be foolish. The best thing to do was to pedal as fast as she could and hope that whoever it was would get tired of their game.

The light on her hands was getting brighter, and her shadow getting more and more pronounced. They were closing the distance. Were they going to hit her? Or would they race around, force her to stop, and do something a lot worse than stealing her bike?

Patricia was gasping now, partly with the effort of pedaling so fast and partly from trying to breathe past the lump of panic in her throat.

Behind her, the truck roared as it accelerated, and she nearly steered the bicycle right into the ditch in fright.

"Patricia!"

She had no idea who it was or why they knew her name. All she knew was that she had to get away. But where? Now the truck was pacing her on the left and there was nothing to her right but the ditch and a barbed-wire range fence. She couldn't stop. She was trapped.

"Patricia, stop!"

Something familiar about that voice finally pierced the miasma of fear that enveloped her. With a gasp, she looked to her left to see a man hanging out of the passenger window, waving both arms in a pressing motion. *Slow down.*

"It's me, Gideon," he shouted. "Stop and we'll give you a ride. It's not safe out here."

A noise came out of her throat halfway between a wheeze and a moan. Both her feet slid off the pedals and she sat back as though her spine had given out, while the bike rolled to a stop. The truck, which she now recognized as Chance Madison's Ford, pulled onto the shoulder ahead of her and stopped, its engine still grumbling.

And suddenly Gideon was at her side, helping her off the bike while holding it with the other hand. *"Bischt du okay?"* he asked urgently. "You're shaking."

"Neh, I'm not okay," she croaked, surprised that her voice even worked. "The two of you just scared me half to death. I thought you were some crazy person who was going to run me off the road."

"I'll put the bike in the back," Chance said, blissfully

unaware she was having a nervous breakdown. He picked it up and lowered it into the bed with some care.

"Don't ever do that to me again," she said to Gideon in *Deitsch*, and jerked her arms out of his grip. "What is the matter with you?"

"I was worried," he said simply. "And glad that Chance was still at the Inn with his truck."

"There was nothing to worry about! I was perfectly fine."

"You don't look fine to me."

She was shaking from head to foot. Tears were leaking from her eyes. Hadn't she'd just told him why she wasn't fine! Or would have been if they hadn't done such a ridiculous thing? Oh, why did she bother?

Patricia hauled open the door of the truck and clambered in. The console that concealed the electronics and had the cup holders in it had been tipped backward to form a middle seat for her. Chance handed her the seatbelt and she clipped it into place with trembling hands.

"Thank you," she managed.

"You okay?"

"I will be. You scared me. I thought it was someone planning to run me off the road."

"I'm sorry about that." She couldn't see his face once Gideon got in and the cab lights shut off. But he sounded sorry. "Let's get you home."

Conversation felt impossible, and she could feel Gideon's agitation. At last he said, "I'm sorry, too, Patricia. Chance had the hazard lights on so that people would see a slow-moving vehicle. When we realized we'd spooked you, that's when he pulled up. We didn't mean to scare you."

"Next time, just let me ride home," she said hoarsely. "But I appreciate the thought." This was more for Chance's benefit than Gideon's, but it would do for both.

The dark landscape whipped by and in two minutes they had reached the King mailbox.

"Here okay?" Chance, it seemed, was learning. A week ago he'd have pulled into the yard and caused a ruckus when her parents came outside and saw her get out.

"Thanks." She unclipped the seatbelt and Gideon slid out to help her down from the high cab. She ignored him and did her two-step process herself.

"I'll walk you up to the house."

"*Neh, denki.* Just get my bike, please."

For once, he didn't argue. He lifted her bike out of the bed in silence and waited until she had mounted. "*Guder nacht.*"

"*Guder nacht.* Thank you, Chance."

"Anytime, Patty."

She wished he wouldn't call her Patty. But she was too drained even to correct him. All she could do was pedal up the lane and over to the barn, where she leaned the bike on the big door. Then she pressed her back to the planks, which were still warm from the heat of the day, and simply breathed. The sounds of the farm at night settled around her—horses blowing gently, the chickens making the occasional sleepy remark, the whisper of the breeze in the pasture grass.

She'd never been so frightened before in her life. Not even that time on the combine.

But she was home now. Home and safe, because of the actions of two boys who thought they were doing the right and gallant thing. She'd come *this close* to tearing a yard of skin off them for scaring her so badly, when really, if a diesel rig *had* come roaring down the county highway, the pickup would have protected her.

Maybe she wouldn't be too hard on Gideon the next time she saw him. Maybe he was a little like Calvin—his heart in the right place but his actions not quite lined up. But she was a fine one to talk. Her heart didn't know what it wanted, and her actions showed it.

Measure twice, cut once, her carpenter brothers always said. Clara said that, too, when it came to sewing. Plan out what you're going to do, and you're less likely to have to do it over. Maybe she should listen to her sensible siblings, and think before she acted.

Was it Gideon who had noticed she'd left the Inn tonight, or Chance? No matter—they'd both come to what they thought was her rescue. Maybe she should apologize to Gideon for screeching at him like a blue jay, and at least thank him for the intent behind his actions.

The Amish tended to believe that actions spoke louder than words. Words vanished on the wind, but actions left results you could touch and remember. As she pushed off the barn door and walked slowly toward the farmhouse, Patricia had the uncomfortable feeling that if anybody's actions should vanish on the wind, it was her own.

12

Saturday, August 13

SINCE BETH STOLZFUS worked with her mother at the quilt shop on Saturdays, Patricia always had the day off. Today she was determined to stay at home and put some thought into planning her new quilt.

"You mean your wedding quilt," Clara said after breakfast and morning chores, joining her in the sewing room. The old Gingerich farmhouse had been built for a family much larger than theirs, so they and Mamm had the luxury of claiming one of the bedrooms upstairs for a sewing room. What a blessing not to have to clear everything away to set the table for meals!

"I thought you said the wedding quilt was sinful," Patricia said, laying out the fabrics she'd prewashed in the bathtub and dried on the line outside. The pattern she'd sketched on graph paper was a modified Hand of Friendship, the blocks both separated and united by sashing and nine-patch blocks. It would be fun to create, and she had a little idea about using different shades of blue and grey to make the design stand out in some areas and fade in others. She was no Malena Miller, but the thought of this orderly design out of her own head made her happy, so at least she shared that with her. Malena was never so happy as when she was sewing ... except, presumably, when she was with the man she loved.

"I didn't say that." Clara was nothing if not precise. "I said a person could look at it that way. I didn't say I did. Mind you, I don't believe a word of Annie's old wives' tale. Even if she's the old wife telling the tale."

"Whether I believe it's going to bring me a husband or not, I'm going to make this quilt." Patricia showed her the sketch. "What do you think? Border or no border?"

Clara studied the penciled blocks and triangles for a moment. "No border," she said at last. "It would take away from it, I think. Close it in when bears are supposed to roam free, claws and all."

"It's a Hand of Friendship. Not a Bear Claw."

Her sister gazed at her, skepticism and disbelief in her eyes. "You don't attract a husband by making a wedding quilt that signifies friendship."

Oh, for goodness sake. "You don't attract one with bear claws, either."

"Unless the man reminds you of a bear."

"Which he doesn't."

Clara pounced. "Who doesn't?"

Patricia resisted the urge to clutch her head and growl like a big brown sow herself. "Nobody. I was speaking in general. I don't know anybody who reminds me of a bear."

"Hmm." Clara, in her usual orderly and maddening fashion, seemed to be running through the roster of available single men in the valley. "Me neither. The closest would be Gideon Miller. He's got thick brown hair like a bear. He's protective, like a sow with cubs. And goodness knows he's got the shoulders and muscles from all that ranch work."

Patricia dropped her sketch on the work table and stared. "Clara King, why are you looking at Gideon Miller's shoulders and muscles, pray tell?"

Her sister shrugged. "Just an observation. Calvin Yoder is built sort of the same, tall and husky, but he's missing the protective part. He can't even protect himself from … himself."

Thankful to guide this swerve in the conversation into less personal channels, Patricia said, "He managed to pull a whole loaf of taffy with you without an accident."

"Only because I kept his attention on the task. That boy now knows as much about making taffy as I do, or Mamm does. He's not as clueless as people think. He's really pretty smart. He just has a hard time keeping his mind on something."

"Even walking," Patricia said. "I wonder if he's dumped himself off his bicycle yet."

"Don't be mean. Which reminds me, he wanted me to ask if I could borrow yours this afternoon, so I could ride over to the state park with him."

This second shock in two minutes left Patricia bereft of words. "He asked you on a *date?*" she finally managed. "And you're only telling me now?"

"No, he asked me to ride to the park," Clara said patiently. "He's got a delivery to make at the bishop's. I was thinking I'd pack a snack and something to drink."

Well, if this didn't cap the globe. But to tease Clara about it would only make her clam up, and then she'd never get the details when the world's most unlikely pair got home.

Instead, Patricia pulled over her tub of fat quarters and then got out the rotary cutter and cutting mat. And in the camaraderie—"Measure twice, cut once," they said together—the entire idea of bear claws and Gideon Miller sank into the sea of forgetfulness.

The image of those broad shoulders and protective arms, however, did not. And the more Patricia tried not to think of them, the more they kept popping up. Reaching for the horse's harness. Serving up supper. Snatching her *Kapp* off the road at a dead run.

She forced her mind to discipline itself and focus on the math of cutting the triangles that would make a series of three-inch finished Hand of Friendship squares.

Bear Claws. Hmph.

THAT AFTERNOON, AFTER CLARA PEDALED OFF TO MEET Calvin at the Wengerd place, Patricia baked a pan of oatmeal fudge bars, the ancient recipe for which was kept in Mamm's tin recipe box where all the family favorites lived. When the pan cooled, she cut the bars, arranged half of them on a plate, and took them over to Aendi Annie.

"Mm," Annie said, savoring the first bite. "As tasty as I ever made them. Did you use my recipe?"

"Of course." Patricia poured them both a cup of coffee with cream, the way they both liked it. "You'll be happy to know I started my quilt. Clara and I did all the cutting this morning."

"I'm glad to hear it. Where did she pedal off to? You've started a fashion, *Liewi*."

"She and Calvin are riding over to the state park."

Annie's eyebrows rose. "My grand-niece? And Calvin Yoder?"

Patricia was glad to know that she wasn't the only one who

could be flummoxed by news this unlikely. "According to your grand-niece, it is. I don't dare say a thing. You know her."

"I want every single detail when they get back, unless she tells you in confidence."

Patricia had to smile. Annie might be in her nineties, but in some ways talking to her was like talking to one of her own buddy bunch. "I'll be sure to—" The rattle of a buggy coming up their short lane made her forget what she was going to say.

"Who can this be?" Annie said, craning to see out the screen door. "Is that the bishop?"

The buggy was very plain, and had none of the dingle-dangles and reflectors stuck on in a pattern, like some of the young men's buggies had. But Little Joe's six-foot-seven-inch frame was unmistakeable when he slid out and tied his horse to the rail in front of the farmhouse. Something about the no-nonsense way he moved made Patricia uneasy.

"Aendi, I think something's happened. We weren't expecting a visit."

"Maybe not. He might just want a word with your father about the hay."

But when Mamm hurried out of the kitchen and across the yard a few minutes later, her eyes were worried. "Patricia, *kumm mit*. The bishop asks you to join us."

"Me?" There could only be one reason for it. Her stomach did a sickening flip. She hadn't had that bicycle for twenty-four hours and now the bishop was on the doorstep. At least the bike was gone with Clara. She'd heard of elders in other districts going so far as to hurl cell phones in the river and direct boys wanting to be baptized to rip the stereo speakers out of their buggies and destroy them.

"Yes, you. *Kummst du jetzt*."

Aendi Annie was not to be left behind—she took Patricia's

arm and, while they walked across the grass, and squeezed it for moral support.

In the kitchen, Patricia sank into her usual chair while Mamm seated her aunt and made sure everyone had coffee and an oatmeal fudge bar from the second plate that hadn't even made it into the refrigerator yet. After he had taken the obligatory bite, Little Joe put down his bar and cleared his throat.

"I had a couple of visitors a little while ago," he began. "They came rolling into our yard on bicycles instead of in a buggy. Can't say I've ever seen such a thing here before."

Silence fell, until Patricia realized he was waiting for her to say something. "My sister said Calvin had a delivery for you."

"That he did."

"And afterward they were riding out to the state park for a picnic."

"So they said. While Calvin was pulling his bicycle out of Sadie's crysanthemum bed."

Ach, neh. "He ran the bike into her flowerbed?" Honestly, could the man not control himself?

"I think he thought there was some sort of stand on it, and maybe there was, but the ground was soft from just being watered and the thing went over into the flowers."

"I'm sure he'll make it up to Sadie somehow," Annie said.

Feeling anxious but unwilling to ask herself why, Patricia added, "Calvin never means to be destructive."

"The point is, there were bicycles in my yard where there never have been before. I understand that you're the instigator of this new fashion, Patricia."

Her cheeks burned with the color flooding into them. "Clara was riding my bike today. A couple of the other *Youngie* saw it last night, and bought one. They had them at the feed store." Inspiration struck. "I hear they're sold out now." No more bicycles—no more problem, *nix?*

"Only because the Eicher boys bought the last two."

Oh.

"What disturbs me is that no one thought to ask themselves whether this new mode of transportation was a *gut* idea. And they certainly never thought to ask anyone else, like a parent or an elder."

"It's just a bicycle," Patricia whispered. "A way to get around."

"We have ways to get around that have served our folk pretty well for three hundred years," Little Joe said. He wasn't shouting—in fact, his voice was more of a quiet, kitchen-table level rumble. But to Patricia, it sounded like Gabriel's trumpet, about to announce her doom.

"They ride bicycles in Pinecraft," she offered. "I didn't think it was important enough to ask permission for."

"Maybe not permission. Call it ... consultation," Little Joe said. "Because transportation is important. It usually involves technology. *Englisch* technology. And bicycles have gears these days. Like cars. Would you say a car was just a way to get around?"

That was hardly fair. Of course it was, technically. But she knew as well as he did there was more to it than that. *"Neh."*

"My counterparts in Lancaster County have already dealt with this troublesome question. And their response was *neh* as well. The *Ordnung* in Whinburg Township and other places in Lancaster County, for instance, allows a push scooter, but it has neither gears nor brakes. Just human feet to make it go and stop. Don't you think that's more becoming to a member of the *Gmay?* More in keeping with our ways?"

A possible escape route shone into Patricia's mind. "But I'm not a member of the *Gmay*."

The bishop took another bite of the oatmeal fudge bar, then finished off the whole thing. "True. But your influence seems to have affected those who are."

Clara. Calvin. The Eicher boys, too. They'd all been baptized and committed to living under the *Ordnung*. Except bicycles weren't in the *Ordnung*.

Yet.

She didn't dare speak again. Speaking might be misconstrued as arguing, and she could never do that. Not with the bishop, and in front of her parents to boot.

Dat stirred in his chair. "*Mei Dochder* will take that bicycle back to the feed store and get a refund."

Neh—that bicycle meant her freedom. A tiny measure of independence and choice. "Dat—"

He held up a hand. "I know. You're on *Rumspringe*. But any behavior that brings the bishop to our home can't be allowed to go on. You'll take it back on Monday."

"But Dat, how am I going to get to work?"

"The same way you did before. Clara can take you to the quilt shop, and on days we don't need the buggy, you can drive yourself."

"I still need to get from the Rocking Diamond to town. Clara's made it plain she doesn't like interrupting her work to hitch up and fetch me. That's why the bicycle—"

"You don't work at the Rocking Diamond any more," her father said heavily.

"I took back my notice yesterday. Mrs Madison is happy to keep me on—it would have been bad for the business to lose me during high season."

Dat's face flushed the way it did when he was trying to

control his temper at this fresh disobedience. Especially with Little Joe to witness it.

A soft answer turneth away wrath.

"I'm on *Rumspringe*, Dat," she said gently. "It's just a job, but it pays well, and I give half to you and Mamm, don't I?"

He didn't reply. Instead, he and the bishop locked eyes, as though it were going to take the two of them to rein her in.

"It could be worse," the bishop said at last.

And there was the truth behind her father's tight hand on the reins. His fear. The spectre of Andrew's two successful attempts to jump the fence—not only leaving home, but actually leaving the state. Not communicating for months, her mother's tears, Dat's grim face and weight loss—oh yes, no one was about to forget any of that.

"So this bicycle is mainly used to get to work?" Little Joe asked.

Dared she hope he might reconsider? "*Ja*, mostly." She didn't have the courage to look up in case she saw the doubt return to his eyes. "I felt I was burdening Clara and the folks on the Rocking Diamond, always needing a ride everywhere. The bicycle gets me to work and back, and then sometimes to a volleyball game, if they're close to town. At least, it could. I haven't really thought much past getting to work."

Little Joe gave a thoughtful nod. "As she says, *Rumspringe*," he said to Dat. "The Petersheim boy, too. Considering they haven't gone off and bought cars and taken the driving test, it seems harmless enough ... for a season."

I'll say. A bicycle is about the most harmless thing in this valley. But Patricia knew better than to say such a thing aloud.

"And the others, who are church members?" Dat asked.

"I'll have to meet with the elders. Maybe even write to some of the other bishops who have dealt with this. But it won't hurt to let the *Youngie* know that it's under consideration, and the other four may have to return their bicycles in the end." His gaze flicked to Patricia. "When your sister comes home, you might mention it to her."

Wordlessly, Patricia nodded.

"Gut." The bishop pushed away from the table and rose. "Thank you for *Kaffee*, Kate. Are all your lambs coming home to roost tomorrow for dinner, along with us?"

"Ja, bishop," Mamm said, her voice hoarse. Likely she hadn't recovered from the reference to Andrew. "I'm making my ham and broccoli casserole, and a tri-tip for the barbecue."

"We'll look forward to that."

No way was Patricia staying in the kitchen to hear what her parents had to say about all this. Aendi Annie had risen, too, so Patricia practically leaped to her side to help her back to the *Daadi Haus*.

They shook hands with Little Joe, and made their slow way across the lawn.

"You had a narrow escape there," Annie murmured. "So did your bicycle. Best keep it strictly for work, and go with Clara or Simeon and Susan to the *Youngie*'s doings. Little Joe will appreciate your obedience."

It was *gut* advice. If she were baptized and a full member of the church.

But she was on *Rumspringe*, and making her own choices was part of it. Not ... obedience.

❧ 13 ❧

Off Sunday, August 14

UNDER NORMAL CIRCUMSTANCES, Patricia loved a summer barbecue, especially with Noah and Rebecca joining them. She even liked to see Susan Bontrager, if only because she made Simeon happy, and a happy Sim was a wonder to behold. But on this off Sunday in the middle of August, she felt out of sorts with her family, as though she had grown a couple of extra kinks that no longer allowed her to fit in.

Only a crazy person would turn down Dat's barbecued tri-tip, however, or Mamm's ham and broccoli casserole with cheese melting both inside and out. Rebecca had brought a tomato and cucumber salad fresh from the Circle M garden, tangy with little Greek olives and lemon dressing. And Susan brought two deep-dish fruit pies that she served with vanilla ice cream.

People ate off their laps in folding chairs or at the picnic table under the apple trees. They'd had a couple of visits from other folks in the district earlier, but it was just the family for supper. Even washing the dishes afterward with Clara, normally a time when they caught up with each other, was unusually silent. Clara was often thoughtful, and tonight Patricia was glad of it. She was too full of her dinner to talk, anyway.

When they finished up and joined the others outside, Simeon was telling them they'd completed the forms for the foundation of Zach and Ruby's future home, and expected to pour concrete the following week. Construction talk was completely normal around their house, and Patricia had hammered her share of nails when both time and help were in short supply. But tonight, the long rays of the sun lay across the fields, lengthening the shadows of the fences so they striped the horses grazing close by. The air smelled soft, like fresh-cut hay. Someone up the valley must have taken off their second crop, and the breeze was blowing the scent their way.

The conversation of the others fell to a murmur as she wandered past the garden to where the lawn turned into uncut meadow. She picked a stem of Queen Anne's Lace, then another, and some yarrow to brighten it up a little. They wouldn't last long in the house, these meadow flowers, but they did bring a cheery note to a room.

"Mind if I join you?" Her brother Noah strolled up, his sage-green shirtsleeves rolled up to the elbow. Rebecca had worn a dress, cape, and apron of the same fabric, but she and Mamm were talking with Susan under the apple trees—probably about the wedding.

"It's been a while since we took a walk together," she responded.

"The field path?"

"Sure."

The field path was actually a wagon track used at haying time. It bisected two big hay fields and made a nice walk. "I always think there are so many wildflowers here because everywhere else is so orderly," she said, stooping to pick another lacy head of Queen Anne's Lace, and a couple of royal-blue cornflowers for good measure.

"It does seem like they're doing it on purpose," Noah agreed, "but it's probably just the fertilizer from the horses."

Patricia smiled at her practical brother as they walked in the wheel tracks, the flowers and long grasses brushing at her skirts.

"I hear you're being a bit of a wildflower yourself," he went on.

She rolled her eyes. "Who have you been talking to? Gideon Miller?"

"*Neh*. Clara. Is it really true she went on a date with Calvin Yoder?"

"A bike ride isn't really a date, but it's true they went yesterday. She borrowed mine. Which turned out to be *gut*, because the bishop came for a visit."

From her tone, Noah would know immediately that it wasn't just an ordinary *I was in the neighborhood* kind of visit. More like a *visitation*.

"He's not happy about the bicycles," Noah guessed. "Is he going to forbid them?"

"Not right away. He has to take advice from the elders, and maybe even some other bishops. But it seems I'm going to be allowed to ride mine to work."

"Well ... that's something. Though I don't see what's wrong with a buggy."

"Ask Clara. She has plenty of opinions about carting me all

over the valley when she's trying to get things done in the house. The point is, I'm on *Rumspringe*, and I need transportation. A bicycle is cheap, you don't have to feed it, and you don't have to bother other people to ride it. It's the perfect solution."

"Until the snow flies," he pointed out.

"I might have to quit the quilt shop, then," she conceded. "No sane person rides a bicycle here in the winter, and Clara is going to be even less impressed about hitching up the buggy in four feet of snow. At least I can snowshoe to the Rocking Diamond."

"The Rocking Diamond." He glanced at her in surprise. They reached the gate, and turned around by mutual accord. "I thought you quit."

"I took it back. I like working there. And even if I have to give up my bike, I can still walk to work. One of the boys has been running me into town for my shift at the quilt shop. Sometimes they even give me a lift in the morning."

"They? Gideon says Taylor Madison laid down the law to Chance, and he's to leave you alone."

"Must not have been much of a law," she said, that out-of-sorts feeling rising inside her again. "He came to the do-over taffy pull at the Inn on Friday." She told him about the scare those *Narre* had given her on the county highway. "I nearly ran off the road from fright."

He gave a low whistle. "Do Mamm and Dat know?"

"*Neh*, they do not, and you're not going to tell them. It turned out to be nothing. Just a pair of boys trying to help and not thinking about how it felt from a girl's point of view."

"But it's a sign, *Schweschder*," he said slowly. "A sign that maybe it would be best to stay out of Chance Madison's way."

"What about Gideon Miller's way?" she demanded. "He was half at fault."

"But he's Amish," Noah said simply.

"Does that make him an angel of light? I'm telling you, Noah, Chance has helped me a lot more than Gideon ever has. He gives me rides even when I know he has other things to do and it's an inconvenience. He never judges me. And he certainly never tells me what to do, like *some* people."

"Nobody's telling you what to do," he said in that soothing tone that worked as well on poultry and baby animals as it did on irritated sisters. "Nothing wrong with being concerned, though. It's never *gut* to get too friendly with the *Englisch*. Especially with those boys." He shook his head. "Joshua's told me a story or two about the trouble he got into with them while he was on *Rumspringe*. He was lucky to escape with his hide."

"Well, I'm not about to go on drinking binges or all-nighters to Whitefish." She'd heard a tale or two from Malena and Rebecca about their youngest brother, too. "Which is why it makes me mad when Dat makes such a fuss over a simple ride to town. Chance is always a gentleman, even if the other two wouldn't know good manners if they tripped over them in broad daylight. I trust him. Besides, even you would have to admit that his truck is a lot more comfortable than any buggy."

"Maybe," Noah said after a moment. "But remember what Isaiah says—*Woe to them that go down to Egypt for help; and stay on horses, and trust in chariots.*"

She blew out a breath of impatience as they reached the gate that would let them back into the yard. She was trying to manage her life and he was quoting an ancient prophet as though chariots weren't closer to buggies than cars were?

"I remember," she managed to reply in a tone that was almost sisterly. "I'm going to walk a little longer, Noah. I need to work off that supper."

"Want me to take in your flowers?"

She'd forgotten they were in her hand. She handed them over and before he'd fairly got his fingers around them, she'd set off down their lane to the road. She wasn't sure which direction she'd turn when she got there, but either way would do. As long as it was away.

They lived between Joshua and Sara Miller's hay farm and the county highway, the latter of which seemed like a *gut* direction to go. It was the way she took to get to work at the Rocking Diamond, and gave her about a mile's scenic walk along part of the Siksika River. More than a year ago, Rebecca had rescued a man near the bridge who turned out to be Patricia's lost brother Andrew. What a crazy time that had been. More than a year later, the air felt lazy with warmth, but the river was still as energetic and noisy as ever. Off to the south, it flattened out in the meadows below the Circle M and settled into lazy sweeps around marsh grass, willow, and sandbars. But here it was rocky and rushing in its hurry to get there.

She passed the *Schulhaus* on the other side of the road, and then her feet made hollow sounds on the pedestrian boardwalk on one side of the bridge as she walked to the middle, leaned on the wooden rail, and gazed down into the water. Trout fanned in the current, and dragonflies dipped and danced in the air, just out of their reach.

A car full of tourists passed, two teenagers wide-eyed and pointing for the others to look at her. She waved, and everyone faced forward with a jolt, as if they'd done something rude. She had to smile. There hadn't been this many tourists in Kentucky, that was for sure and certain. Here the numbers were increasing, and to be honest, Mountain Home had begun to prosper because people were coming to see the Amish, interested in their ways. But from what she'd heard, nothing could touch the number of tourists in places like Ohio or Lancaster County, all interested in the Amish. What must it be like to live under such constant scrutiny, while trying to manage work and church and family?

The slow beat of boots on the boards at the *Schulhaus* end of the bridge made her look up. Gideon Miller waved and she let out a breath, wondering for one wild moment if Noah had called him to check up on her.

"Hallo," he said, leaning on the rail a few feet away and taking a moment to inspect the trout, just as she'd done. "I was on my way over to your place and saw you." He hesitated. "Unless you'd rather be alone?"

It would be rude to say yes, so she shook her head. "I needed a walk. It's fine. You're fine." *Stop babbling. He can look at the fish if he wants.*

"I hear the bishop came by yesterday."

Good grief. There was nothing more efficient than the Amish grapevine. "He did."

"About the bicycles?"

"Of course. What else?"

"Well, you're going on *Rumspringe*. He might have wanted to offer you some counsel."

"*Neh*, it was about the bicycle." She gave him the gist of the bishop's errand, a little bit tired of repeating it. "But I'm not living under the *Ordnung* yet. He can't really tell me I can't ride to work on my own bike until I join church."

"I bet he made his preference known, though."

"So did Dat. But it's not up to them, is it?"

He gazed into the rush of the river without replying. "I

wonder how many people have stood right here and wondered where the water would take them if they just waded in and swam with it."

Gideon Miller, waxing philosophical? Wonders never ceased. But better to talk philosophy than to wonder what those broad shoulders would look like if he went swimming. "You mean, besides through the Circle M land and into the lake?"

His lips tipped up in a smile. "Besides that. I guess that's the nature of rivers. Taking people places, I mean." He glanced at her curiously. "Do you ever think of leaving?"

She relaxed into her original study of the water, too, elbows on the rail, hands loosely clasped. If he hadn't come looking for her to start an argument, she could choose the better part and meet him halfway. Have a rational conversation that would chase away the pictures in her head.

"Sometimes. Then I think of my parents and what it did to them when Andrew left—both times—and the idea fades away."

"Noah's told us some of what it was like for him," he said soberly, watching the trout. "Also a little of what he went through when he thought Rebecca was going to marry Andrew. What a strange situation."

"But like the Scripture says, all things work together for good to them who love God."

"Don't forget the second part. *And are called according to His purpose.* That was the thing with Andrew. He never accepted the call, or *Gott's* purpose for his life. So he ran away. To Colorado, to the ski hills. Then here." He hooked a thumb in the direction of the steeply sloping bank to their right. "Literally here. That's where Rebecca pulled him out. She showed me once. Right by that clump of willows."

She hadn't known the exact location. She gazed at it, wondering how on earth slender, blonde Rebecca could have managed such a feat where the bank was so steep. But if Andrew had been called according to *Gott*'s purpose, He must have given her the strength.

"Is your brother going to join church for good and all?" Gideon asked. "Isn't he courting the sister of our Adam's Kate, out east?"

"He was," she said slowly. "But I think there might be a fly in the ointment. Something in a letter from our cousin Carrie Miller in Whinburg made Mamm look a little worried and write back right away. We haven't heard from Andrew—or Elizabeth. I don't know what's going on. What about you?" she asked, to bring the subject back where it belonged. "Do you want to wade into the river and see where it goes?"

He chuckled and shook his head. "Not me. This place is home. I knew it the minute we got off the train in Libby and I looked up at all those mountains. The air was colder in February than I ever knew air could be, and yet I wanted to just stand there on the platform, looking up, drinking it in."

"Mamm is like that, too. She spent her summers here with Aendi Annie and Onkel Jess, and fell in love with the Siksika. That's why we moved here."

"I thought it was to look after Annie. She's the oldest person in the *Gmay*, though you'd never know it."

"It was," she agreed. "But mostly it was Mamm, wanting to come back to the mountains. Annie was the reason she needed to make it happen, and then of course, Annie's offering her and Dat the farm was the icing on the cake."

The river chuckled and laughed fifteen feet below them. Another car passed, but Patricia was barely aware of it. "Did you take a *Rumspringe*?" she asked him.

"Oh, sure. But it didn't last long. I knew I was going to join church. Mostly it was to keep Seth company, though goodness knows there wasn't much in the way of worldly entertainment in the Ventana Valley in New Mexico. We wound up being baptized the same Sunday, after Dat died. And then the families started moving away."

"So ... you just knew that you were going to join church. The way you knew the Siksika was the place for you?" She sighed. "I wish I was like that."

"Maybe you are, deep down," he suggested. "If you're not looking at bus schedules and wondering how your buddy bunch is doing in Kentucky, then maybe you've already decided in your heart, even if it hasn't told you yet."

She frowned at him. "I was just thinking about my buddy bunch, in fact. Maybe it's time to start a circle letter."

"Maybe," he said easily. "My sister writes to people all the time, though she never really had a buddy bunch. Not enough girls her age in the Ventana. Did you meet our cousin Emily Kuepfer at Christmas?"

"*Ja*. I liked her. Do she and Susanna write?"

He nodded. "I wonder if she and Stephen will visit Prince Edward Island on their honeymoon trip, after they see the family in Whinburg Township."

"It's an awfully long way."

"A couple thousand miles, I think. Too far for me. But Seth talks about it once in a while. We have a standing invitation out there."

"I can't imagine going so far. The trip from Kentucky to here was plenty long enough for me."

"New Mexico to here was enough for me, and it's not even half as far as you came." He smiled at the trout, then over at her. "Emily told us about a Scottish woman who was supposed to come and settle in Montreal. She was so seasick that when she got off the boat in Charlottetown, she said, 'Here I am, and here I stay.' That's how I feel."

"And you're not even seasick," she teased.

"Not even when I get stuck riding Chrysanthemum. His gait would make anybody sick. I've just learned to roll with it."

Now it was her turn to laugh. "Here you are, and here you'll stay. With, I suppose, a special someone, someday."

"I suppose," he agreed, gazing out over the river. "But I'm not in any hurry. When *Gott* wills it, it'll happen."

"According to Aendi Annie, when our family needs more help than *Gott* provides, there's always the wedding—"

She'd meant to laugh about a tradition that seemed more optimism than reality. But somehow, despite the fact that they'd been talking for half an hour without breaking into a fight, the King family folklore felt just a little too intimate for sharing. He might get the idea a quilt was bringing *them* together, and that would never do.

She pressed her lips together and let the river chuckle in the silence.

"The wedding what?" he prompted after a moment.

"Oh ... nothing. It's silly."

"All right," he said, nodding. "I can always ask Aendi Annie."

Good gracious. Even worse. "It's just a funny family tradition. Annie says that when a King *Maedsche* begins her wedding quilt, she meets the man she's going to marry by Christmas of the same year."

To her relief, he laughed, giving the notion exactly the consideration it deserved. "Please don't tell me Clara started her quilt this year. Not with Calvin in the picture."

She pretended to bury her face in her hands. "Oh, no. Not

that. Anything but that." Then she laughed, too. "So far, *neh,* she hasn't. But there are four months left yet."

"And what about yours?"

Well, goodness, why shouldn't she tell him? It wasn't like *he* was *Gott*'s choice for her.

‹§ 14 §›

"I HAVE, in fact, started a queen-sized quilt," Patricia said in a tone that just missed being a challenge. But to him or *der Herr*, Gideon wasn't certain. "Clara and I cut all the fabric yesterday, but I've been buying up quarters and lengths for a while now."

"Uh-oh. Should all the single men be afraid?"

"Afraid of little old me?" She batted her lashes at him and he was surprised into a shout of laughter so unexpected his hat nearly came off and tumbled into the river.

While he was screwing it down on his head, the rumble of a diesel engine and the howl of tires on the bridge bed drowned out the last of his humor. He knew that sound. The very worst sound a man could hear during such an enjoyable moment.

The red pickup pulled up beside them, blocking the eastbound lane completely. Chance Madison lowered the passenger window. "Hey, you two. Long time no see."

Not long enough, if you asked him. "Chance," he greeted the other man. "What are you up to on a Sunday night?" The sun was nearly down, peeking between the pines before it sank altogether behind the mountain range.

"I was just going for a drive. Want to come along?"

Who was he talking to? Both of them? Gideon made a fast decision. "Thanks, but we were just heading over to—"

"Sure," Patricia said brightly. "Meet you on the other side."

Chance nodded and the big truck rumbled on to where the wood and steel barrier that separated people from traffic ended.

"*Guder owed*, Gideon," she said over her shoulder as she walked away.

"Patricia, wait— Are you—? What if—"

But it was too late. Her pace picked up until she was jogging, the white strings of her *Kapp* lifting off her shoulders and fluttering behind her. And before he could get his own feet moving fast enough, she'd reached the truck, climbed in, and slammed the door.

The big vehicle roared as Chance accelerated up the hill out of the cut the river had made, leaving Gideon with nothing but his own surprise and the smell of diesel exhaust hanging in the air.

How could she? They'd been enjoying the evening—well, he had—and joking and laughing together for the first time ever. How could she walk away from that and take up the invitation of a worldly man? Was she trying to prove something to herself? Or simply rubbing his nose in the fact that she could do as she liked regardless of what anyone thought?

Gideon felt sick. But whether it was worry for her alone with a Madison, or disappointment that she'd been so quick to abandon him, he couldn't tell. Probably both. Even the sound of the engine had faded now. They were long gone, headed who knew where. There was nothing out that direction but the state park, and after that the Bitterroot Range and Idaho.

Well, he couldn't stand here all evening waiting for them to come back so he could make sure Patricia was okay. If he had a horse or even a bicycle, he could have ridden out to the state park to check whether the truck was there. But he didn't. And she probably wouldn't thank him for following her if he did.

With a despondent sigh, he turned and headed back to the Circle M, where hopefully he could make it into the bunkhouse unseen by anyone except his brother. But when he passed the path that led from the county highway up over the ridge and behind the Miller house, he thought of a better plan than simply going to bed.

He set off up the trail. At the halfway point he could look down and see Adam's house, lit from within but silent. Likely Adam and Kate were in there, arranging the cabinets that had been ordered but not yet delivered, and moving imaginary furniture in the newly drywalled and plastered rooms.

In a few minutes, Gideon reached his destination—Gross-mammi Miller's orchard, tucked into a box canyon that was just a little warmer and more sheltered than anywhere else on the ranch, enough to give the apples a better chance than apples in Montana usually got in their short growing season. He walked under the trees, inhaling the fragrance of fruit that was nearly ripe, and enjoying the rustle of thick green leaves that hung over them protectively. At the end of the row, some-thing darted through the knee-high grass and vanished. Too small to be a coyote. Maybe a fox.

He leaned on a gnarled trunk and simply breathed, trying to calm his spirit without much success. How could she? The question nagged at him like a mosquito. How could she choose Chance Madison and practically run away from him when they'd been having such a nice time? What had he done wrong?

"Gideon?" came a feminine voice, quiet, but enough to jolt him out of his thoughts. "Is that you?"

"*Ja*, Aendi."

Naomi Miller strolled along the short avenue between the trees, looking as natural and at home in these surroundings as she did in the kitchen or in a corral exercising a horse. "What are you doing up here? I thought I was alone until that fox jumped, and then I saw you farther on."

The last thing he wanted was for his confusion to spoil her refuge. The whole family came to this orchard the way the old hymn said. *To the rock that is higher than I.* "It's nothing," he said. "I'll leave you to your meditation."

With a smile that told him she'd seen right through him, she said, "I find that people come up here not so much to see how the apples are doing—like I am—but when they're rumpled up in their minds. Would it help to talk? Or ... maybe you'd want to do that with your mother."

Mamm was five miles away, and his aunt was right here, her eyes sympathetic. He wasn't in the habit of confiding his troubles and questions to anyone, except maybe Seth or Tobias, if he was really *verhuddelt*. But there was something about his aunt that invited confidences—depths that contained wisdom as well as the ability to submerge a subject and never talk about it with anyone else.

He sighed, and with a tilt of his head indicated a bench that appeared recently. It seemed to have been constructed of leftover house studs and ironwork, and had been set just where a person could look down the avenue of trees and see one of the peaks glowing in the last of the sunlight.

"Reuben and Adam made this and brought it up here last

week," she told him, settling on it. "My husband seems to know without my telling him that in beautiful places, a person needs somewhere to sit while they soak in *Gott*'s goodness. It's just not the same when you have to stand."

"I agree," Gideon said, while his mind whirred, trying to decide whether or not to confide in her. Whether or not there was even anything to confide. And out of his mouth came the words, "Have the Kings ever mentioned a wedding quilt?"

If she wondered where *that* had come from, she didn't betray it. She simply relaxed against the slats of the bench back. "I assume you don't mean the kind that Malena makes?"

"More like a family story."

"*Ja*, sure. Annie Gingerich has mentioned it a time or two at quilting frolics. Seems it's a family tradition. If a woman starts a wedding quilt, she'll meet the man she's going to marry that same year." She paused. "Seems more coincidence than anything. Women tend to make wedding quilts when they reach a certain age and have a certain confidence in a man's intentions. Why?"

"Oh ... I ran into Patricia on the bridge and it came up."

"Did it?" Naomi said in the kind of tone that meant, *The girl is bringing up weddings with you?*

"We were talking. And having fun for once. Mostly she's as prickly as a cactus. Or maybe that's just when she's around me."

"Are you prickly around her?"

"I didn't think so." But he thought about it. "Maybe I'm kind of ... bossy. But I can't help speaking up when she does crazy things." He gestured off to the east. "Like jumping into Chance Madison's truck practically in the middle of our conversation and driving off with him."

Her eyes widened. "Just now? Before you came up here?"

He nodded morosely. "I thought we were having a nice time. But she couldn't seem to get away fast enough. She was almost running."

Naomi turned her gaze to a Steller's jay teetering on a branch. When it realized it was being watched, it squawked and flew away. "Maybe she wasn't running away from you, but from herself."

What did that mean? He glanced at her, feeling as confused as he probably looked.

"I can't speak for her, of course, but you said you were having a *gut* conversation. Fun, even."

"Joking around together. Even about the wedding quilt. I asked her if Clara had started one, and it was clear we both hoped not."

With a flash of a smile, Naomi said, "I heard about her and Calvin. But imagine someone who is set on spreading her wings just a little. Of *Rumspringe*, even if it's only a few months. And here she's finding a friend in an Amish man—someone she can laugh with, which she might not have known before. Someone who is concerned for her—who isn't a member of her family. He and *Rumspringe* might have bumped up against each other down there on the bridge, and she did what many people do."

"She ran."

Naomi was silent, letting that sink in. Then she said, "Do you like her?"

After a moment in which he collected his courage, he nodded. "When she's not mad at me. When I'm not having to rescue her."

"Rescue her? How do you do that?"

"Well, Chance and I did. She was riding her bike home from the taffy pull on the county highway. At the three-mile marker he caught up to her in the truck while I waved out the window and got her to stop so we could put the bike in the bed. She was pretty mad. Said we'd scared her to death. But we were being a barrier behind her, going slow and staying between her and traffic—maybe even a diesel rig."

"Those don't come down the county highway so much anymore."

"Well, you know what I mean." His mind went back to the way they'd laughed together. "She has a great laugh. A sense of humor. A little bent, like she sees things differently. Things are funny to her that aren't to other people."

But Naomi was not, apparently, to be distracted. "I hear Chance has turned up a time or two at the *Youngie*'s doings. Is he coming for her sake, do you think?"

And there it was, right out in the open. "I think so. I don't see it going anywhere good, especially since she's going to keep working at the Rocking Diamond. I don't know, Aendi. It worries me."

"So then maybe what you want to do is find ways to spend a little time with her. If she's with you having fun, she won't be with Chance."

"But he seems to be part of this *Rumspringe* idea."

"I'm pretty sure she knows he can't be part of her life when her *Rumspringe* ends. But if you're more interesting and fun than he is, she'll realize that you can."

"I'm not exactly the interesting and fun type. I ride fence and herd cows and that's about it."

"Your cousins do, too, and *Gott* brought them just the women He wanted for them," she said firmly. "But there's nothing wrong with taking Patricia for an ice cream after her shift at the quilt store. Or asking her to come swimming with your cousins and staying for a barbecue. It's supposed to get pretty hot this week, so we're planning ahead."

"I'll need to borrow a buggy for things like that."

"I'll drop a word in Reuben's ear. We'll make one available for you to take."

He looked at her sideways from under his hat brim. "Are you matchmaking, Aendi Naomi?"

She tilted her chin. "Certainly not. If my nephew wants to help a *Freind* sow some grass seed on this side of the fence rather than looking over it to where the grass seems to be greener, why, I'll do my best to give him a hand in this *gut* and honest work."

He had to laugh. "I can't say I won't be grateful. Not that I have intentions in that direction. But it seems, like you say, to be a *gut* and honest thing to do. What a *Freind* would do."

The two of them left the orchard together. Gideon felt lighter in his spirit than he had in a week. There was something about the orchard—or maybe it was his aunt—that was like a tonic to the soul.

Maybe sometime he could bring Patricia up here so she could experience it, too. Maybe as soon as this week.

WHEN THE RED PICKUP REACHED THE TOP OF THE RIVER CUT and Patricia got herself buckled into the passenger seat, the difference between now and five minutes ago settled on her. Five minutes ago, she'd been laughing with someone who understood what she said—and didn't say. Now, she rode in the comfort of the truck with the windows down, listening to the radio and the highway going by and not saying much of anything.

She had to make an effort, after he'd been kind enough to offer her an outing. "Did you have a good weekend?"

"Not since the taffy party," Chance admitted. "Me and Clint played video games this afternoon. And yesterday I guided a half-day ride. Those aren't very interesting, but at least they're over quick."

"Do you like the longer ones? Isn't the longest five days?"

"Yep. The terrain is higher and rougher, and mostly it's hunters booking those in the fall. I got an elk one year. So did a guy from Boston. Had to helicopter them out."

Patricia tried to imagine what this astonishing feat might entail, but imagination failed her. Time to change the subject. "Where are we headed?"

"I don't know. Where do you feel like going?"

"Well, it's going to be dark soon. We could have gone to the state park, but the gates close at sunset."

"Guess we missed it." He didn't seem too bothered about that. "You and Miller seemed pretty friendly back there."

She shrugged. "We're friends. Most of the Amish kids are. We all know each other."

"I think he's got a thing for you."

"If he does, he's keeping it a deep, dark secret." With a laugh, she went on, "It doesn't matter anyway. I don't have a thing for him." Well, she didn't. Thinking about a man's shoulders and liking his laugh did not constitute a *thing*. As Clara might say, they were simply observations.

Chance turned on the headlights, and a mile marker sign flashed by.

IDAHO 42

"We'd better turn back," she suggested, "unless you want to end up in Idaho."

"What's wrong with that? There's a little town just over the state line that has a great restaurant. Sometimes they have live music on weekends. I've been there a couple of times."

She opened her mouth to protest, and then closed it. She was on *Rumspringe*. Why shouldn't she go to a great restaurant in Idaho? Except she'd left the house only intending to take a walk. "I don't have my purse with me. Or any money."

"You don't need any." He glanced at her and gave the faintest of smiles, as though he didn't do it very often. "My treat."

All right, then. She settled back in the comfortable seat and watched night fall. He turned up the radio and forty-two miles seemed to scroll out behind them like the wake behind a loon or a Canada goose on the river.

At the restaurant, he ordered a steak dinner while she settled for a Caesar salad. "I already ate supper," she told him, "but you go ahead."

"Anything to drink, Mr Madison?" the waitress, who clearly knew him, asked.

"Just water," Patricia said.

"We'll have a bottle of the Duckhorn Merlot."

"Yes, *sir*," the waitress said with a big smile.

Patricia had no idea what that was until a bottle full of purplish wine came and he and the waitress performed the oddest little ceremony she'd ever seen, blowing and swishing the stuff while she did her best not to laugh. She'd seen many a *Kind* disciplined for doing exactly what Chance was doing. Finally he nodded, and the waitress poured two glasses.

"Oh ... no, I can't," she protested.

"Just try a sip. For a hundred bucks I don't want to enjoy it alone."

"You paid *a hundred dollars* for that bottle?" she hissed. "Is it made of gold?"

"Nope. Grapes. Go on, try it."

When was she going to get another chance to try anything this expensive? She took a cautious sip and tasted half a dozen flavors cascading over her tongue. The second sip was just as good. The second glass was better, and she discovered she was having a wonderful time. Chance shared his steak with her, and she shared her salad with him, because the man seemed to be allergic to vegetables. By the time the band mounted the little stage, they were waiting for dessert. Something called *crème brulée* that apparently involved a blowtorch.

The music started up and Chance said, "Want to dance?"

This was hilariously funny. "I'm Amish," she said, as if he didn't know. "I don't know how." Because it was a sin. But the only people who seemed to think that were the Amish. The other couples walking out there didn't.

Out on the dance floor, he held her and swayed back and forth to a country tune she'd never heard but that she decided was now her favorite. He was just the nicest guy and her father and Noah and mostly Gideon Miller were all completely wrong about him.

They shared the *crème brulée,* which had arrived while they were dancing and which turned out just to be custard. But it tasted amazing. With it they had a dessert wine. She'd never known that desserts had their own wines. It was yummy.

It was late when he finally helped her into the truck and they started home. The song they'd danced to came on the radio and she sang along to it. So what if she sounded more like a crow cawing than a proper singer—he didn't seem to care. But oh my, there were sure a lot more curves in the road going west than there had been going east.

"Are we even on the same road?" she gasped as the truck went one way and her stomach another.

"Yep. See?"

Mountain Home 18

"Uhhh—Chance. I don't feel so good." The window slid down like magic and she hung out of it, gulping in deep breaths of air.

The night wind tore off her *Kapp* and sent it pinwheeling off into the dark. "My *Kapp*! Stop! I lost my *Kapp*!"

"I'll buy you another one."

"You don't *buy* them. You *make* them. Stop!"

But he didn't. He didn't even slow down.

"Chance!" And then everything in her stomach reared up and out and she barely got her head out of the window in time.

He jammed his foot on the brake and her body raked forward against the seatbelt, then back. Something disgusting dribbled down the front of her cape and she groaned with humiliation.

"Did you just throw up on my truck?"

"You should have stopped!"

"I swear, Patty, if stomach acid strips the paint—"

"My name is *Patricia* and I want my *Kapp*," she wailed, and burst into tears. This was the absolute worst night of her life and he was so mean she didn't even have words for it.

He reversed and they went wheeling up the highway backward, which made her lunge for the window again. She threw up until there was nothing left—not even the hundred-dollar wine—barely aware that he'd stopped and got out. A bright light shone on the door, but she had her head on her arms in the open window, weeping and hiccuping and hating herself.

He got in and tossed the *Kapp*, now soiled and punched in on one side, into her lap.

She held it in both hands and sniffled and felt sorry for herself for eighteen miles. And after they crossed the bridge and turned left on the road home, they stopped a minute later at the King mailbox. She got out of the truck, barely able to keep her knees steady. She'd shambled halfway up their lane before she realized she hadn't said good night or thank you or anything.

But the rumble of the engine was already fading into the distance.

She had no idea what time it was, but a lamp was still burning in the kitchen. If she'd thought throwing up all over a man's vehicle was bad, the worst was yet to come.

$\mathscr{H}$ 15 $\mathscr{H}$

Monday, August 15, 12:45 a.m.

THROUGH THE WINDOW in the kitchen door, Patricia could see Mamm sitting at the table, reading. When she walked in on a breeze flavored with vomit and wine, her hair coming out of its bob and her dirty *Kapp* dangling from limp fingers, Mamm's eyes widened, her nostrils pinched, and she laid down the book so blindly it was lucky it landed on the table and not the floor.

"Dochsder," she said in a voice so constricted by shock it was almost a whisper, "what happened to you?"

"You shouldn't have waited up," Patricia croaked. Her throat felt raw and raspy. "It's after midnight."

"I didn't know where you were. One minute we were having company and the next we were going to bed and you weren't here. Dat called all the places around us and no one had seen you."

"Gideon Miller did." Of course he had tattled on her.

"The Circle M was the last place he called," her mother

said. "Naomi said you were with Chance Madison." Her voice turned up at the end in a question.

"I don't want to talk about it." She turned for the stairs.

"Kumm, Liewi," Mamm said, crossing the kitchen to slide an arm around her waist. "A hot shower and some toothpaste will work wonders."

Maybe not wonders, but being clean went a long way. Afterward, she sat in the spindle chair in her room while Mamm combed out her hair the way she used to when Patricia was little, the long strokes relaxing her once the tangles were out.

"Chance took you to a bar?" Mamm asked at last.

She shook her head, and the strokes resumed their leisurely rhythm. "A restaurant over the state line. He ordered wine, and we danced, and I threw up out the window all over his truck. Then he got mad at me."

"At least he brought you home."

She supposed she ought to be grateful for that. She might still be in Idaho, walking those forty-two miles.

"Am I in trouble, Mamm?" Weeks of doing all Clara's chores on top of her own on top of her two jobs loomed in her future. Exhaustion at the thought made her shoulders slump.

"Not now." A tiny thread of humor made its way into Mamm's voice. "I think you found a more effective way of punishing yourself than anything I could think of. There. You're done. Want me to braid it?"

She nodded, like the little *Maedsche* she used to be. Mamm's fingers were gentle as she divided her hair in half, then wove two French braids down the back of Patricia's head, all the way to the ends at her waist.

"Think you'll go out with Chance again?"

Not for the rest of eternity. She shook her head.

Mamm kissed the part on top of her head and silently left the room, taking Patricia's soiled *Kapp* with her.

IN THE MORNING, CLARA PEEKED IN THE DOOR. "PATRICIA? It's time to get up. I'm starting breakfast."

Patricia groaned as each word fell on her brain like a hammer. "I'm sick."

"Sick how?"

"Flu." As if to prove it, her stomach rolled and she bolted past her sister to the bathroom. But someone was in there—someone male—Sim or Dat—oh help—

She dove into the nearest room, snatched up the wastebasket, and vomited the last evidence of the previous evening into it.

"Patricia, good grief, go back to bed," Clara said in horror. "I'll manage breakfast."

Everyone in the house had to stick their head in after that, and found her burrowing deeper under the quilt to get away from both questions and light.

It wasn't until Mamm came in and said, "*Liewi*, should I send Clara over to the Rocking Diamond to tell them you're sick?" that she realized two things simultaneously.

If she didn't go to work, they'd think she'd changed her mind again and quit.

And she had to be hungover. She'd only ever heard about it. No one had ever told her it was this awful. She was never going to touch a drop of alcohol again.

"A glass of water?" she croaked. She downed it and the volume of pain seemed to decrease a little. "I'm getting up."

"Are you sure?" Mamm went out and refilled the glass.

"If I don't show up, they'll think I quit after all. I have to go."

The green dress she'd worn last night had vanished, too, because Mondays were laundry day. She had an old purple one with a black cape and apron that would have to do. It wasn't nearly as pretty, but cleaning rooms didn't require pretty. Besides, putting one foot in front of the other to walk the mile or so to the dude ranch was all she could manage today. Pretty was out of the question.

When she got to the Rocking Diamond, she managed to avoid being seen by just about everyone except Zefra.

"You look awful," her boss said, the blunt words softened by sympathy. "If you're sick, you'd better turn around and go home."

"Not sick." Patricia couldn't bring herself to say anything more. Her head wobbled on her neck like a baby's.

"Too much fun with Chance last night?"

She hurt too badly to care how on earth she knew that. "Maybe."

Zefra squeezed her shoulder. "Drink lots of water. Dehydration makes it worse. And you can start in Cabin Ten. Nice and dim in there, with all the trees. I'll run interference for you until you feel better."

The understanding in her voice nearly brought Patricia to tears.

When the world's longest shift ended at noon, she was beginning to feel more like a human being instead of something on the bottom of a horse's hoof. Thank goodness she didn't have to work at the quilt shop today—they were closed Sundays and Mondays. The laundry would be done by the time she got home, and the prospect of maybe putting in a couple of hours on her quilt made a bright spot in a day that she couldn't wait to put behind her.

Clara was waiting on the King porch when Patricia emerged from the lane, her eyes wide, practically bouncing on her toes. "You have to see this!" Her sister clutched her arm as she gained the porch. "I've never seen anything like it, even at a wedding. Come and see!"

She dragged Patricia into the kitchen. Mamm turned from the casserole she'd just taken out of the oven to watch. Patricia stopped dead, her eyes practically falling out of her head at what sat on the table neatly laid for lunch.

A fountain of flowers exploded out of a knobbly glass vase in every color of the sunset—scarlet, gold, orange, and at least six different shades of pink. Bird of paradise, roses, stargazer lilies, freesia, and gerbera daisies were set off by fern and salal and something broad-leaved she couldn't identify. The thing was at least three feet tall.

"What on earth ...?" she managed.

"Here's the card." Clara pushed a tiny envelope into her hand. "We're dying to know who it's from."

Why did they think it was for her? If it was actually for Clara—and Calvin had sent it—she was never going to let her live it down.

But no. PATTY KING had been written on the envelope in neat capitals. It had been sent by the only florist in Mountain Home, which was a tiny shop. This bouquet had probably cleaned them out of their entire stock.

At a loss, Patricia slid out the card.

THANKS FOR LAST NIGHT. I HAD A GOOD TIME.
TRUCK IS OK. HOPE YOU FEEL BETTER.
CHANCE

Wordlessly, she handed it to Clara, who read it and gave it to Mamm. "Well, I'm glad *he* had a *gut* time," her sister said. "Did you?"

"I don't want to think about it. Mamm, we have to get this off the table before—"

Too late. The kitchen door opened and Dat came in from the barn. His reaction was the same as Patricia's. In the silence, she took the opportunity to lift the tropical explosion off the table and carry it into the living room, where it couldn't be seen from Dat's chair. Mamm quietly explained who it was from, and he was reading the card when Patricia returned.

"Were you feeling poorly, *Dochder*?" he finally asked, as though this might be the most sensible thing to start with.

"*Ja*, Dat. I'm better now."

"And what happened to his truck?"

"He thought some of the paint might have been damaged, but I guess not."

"And why should you care about damage to Chance Madison's truck? Was there an accident?"

"Arlon, lunch is getting cold," Mamm said. "Let us sit and say grace."

Any hopes that Mamm might have quietly told him the story later vanished as soon as they raised their heads. Within five minutes, her father had the whole sad tale out of her—as much as she could remember, anyway. She could hardly bear the look of disappointment in his eyes. It had been a long time since she'd seen the kind of sorrow in his face that Andrew had once put there regularly.

"Dat, I'm so sorry," she finished. "It will never happen again, I promise."

"And from the state of her when she came in last night, Arlon, you can believe that the consequences have been as painful as they were appropriate. We will not speak of it again." Mamm addressed her meal, the subject now closed.

Patricia resumed normal breathing. But the flowers still remained to be dealt with. What on earth was she to do with them?

"I can't keep them here," she said to Clara as they climbed the stairs to the sewing room. "What if some of the *Gmay* come to visit? People are in and out all the time, and *that's* certainly no bouquet of wildflowers gathered on the side of the road."

"Keep them in your room?" Clara seated herself at one of their two treadle sewing machines and picked up the next group of strips for the Log Cabin she was working on. She had them all laid out on the floor and worked through them a square at a time.

Patricia took the strips for the nine-patch daisies and sat down at the other machine. "Then there wouldn't be room for me."

"Break it down. Toss out those ugly pointy ones and some of the greenery, and make smaller bouquets. If we don't have enough vases, we can ask Aendi Annie for some. "

Patricia lined up two strips and began to sew, her spirits lightening. "*Gut* idea. She would love the roses, wouldn't she? And Mamm likes those colored daisies—maybe she'd like some on the kitchen windowsill."

"You can put the freesia and lilies in my room. They smell wonderful."

The bouquet began to feel less like a burden and more of a way to give small pleasures to the women in her family. "Whatever is left will go in the compost, where no one can see it."

They bent to their work and in a couple of hours Patricia had sewn and cut dozens of strips to form the daisies. She wasn't like Clara, laying them out in orderly piles, but they were so straightforward she could leave one big pile next to the cutting mat for their next quilting day.

Then she had the pleasure of disassembling the bouquet and turning it into something people could actually live with. She put some of the roses in her room, and carried the rest over to Aendi Annie—and what a difference to see someone's eyes widen with pleasure rather than shock!

"Are those for me?"

Patricia had to laugh. "I hope you have a vase big enough."

"Oh yes indeed. Many of our wedding presents didn't survive small children and large worship gatherings, but a couple of the vases did. Let me get one out of the *Eck*."

Once arranged in the white milk-glass vase, the roses really did look pretty. As if they belonged on Annie's small kitchen table with its dark green cloth.

"I saw the delivery van," Annie said. "Were they bringing these?"

"They brought a monstrosity as big as a small child. Clara and I have been sharing the wealth. I'm glad you like them, Aendi."

"And who sent them, might I ask?"

She'd only find out from Mamm, so Patricia repeated the whole embarrassing story, down to the contents of the card.

"It's nice to know he values his truck as much as your well-being," Annie said, her tone flavored with just a hint of lemon.

"I'm just glad I don't have to pay to have the door repainted. I have no idea how much that would be, but it has to be a lot. That truck is pretty new."

"At least he got you home in one piece. If he was drinking, too, I shudder to think what might have happened."

"Not as much as me," Patricia said in a low voice, remembering careening up the highway backward. "I am never drinking again. It was awful. And I promised Mamm I wouldn't go out with him again, either."

"He'll ask, *Liewi*."

"Then I'll have a reason why I can't."

"Such as ...?"

Patricia waved her hands as if dozens of reasons stood around her. "Like I have to do the laundry, or the baking, or sewing. And if that doesn't work, I'll say I'm expected elsewhere and close the door."

"Those might be all right," Annie said thoughtfully. "Though he does tend to turn up at places where you're expected."

That was true. "What do you think I should do?"

Annie's lips twitched. "Take up with an Amish boy, the sooner the better."

"Oh, very funny. Be serious, Aendi."

"I am." Annie's eyes sure did look serious, magnified as they were by the lenses of her glasses. "When Chance asks you, say you're doing something with Gideon. When you're out and about in town, make sure it's with Gideon. When you're off shift, Gideon can see you home."

Patricia was already shaking her head *and* waving her hands, as though the reasons had turned into a swarm of bees. "Wait, wait, wait. What has Gideon Miller to do with anything?"

"You said you and he were talking down on the bridge when all this started."

"*Ja*, but—"

"He's the only young man you've given two minutes to lately. He's from a *gut* family, and goodness knows if a young woman needed a nice-sized man between herself and someone she wanted to get rid of, Gideon would do admirably."

It was a few seconds before Patricia could get her mouth to work. Even then, all that came out was, "Aendi!"

"Mark my words," her great-aunt said with imperturbable calm, touching one of the roses as gently as if it were Patricia's cheek. "Gideon Miller is the solution to this whole problem."

$\approx$ 16 $\approx$

THE ORDNUNG in the Siksika Valley had evolved over the fifty years since the Amish had begun to settle there to be less a rejection of *Englisch* ways—though there was plenty of that— than an adaptation to the necessities of ranch life. In many Amish communities, riding the buggy horses or even horses trained to the saddle was forbidden. But in ranch country, a man rode a horse as part of his business on the range, in the protection of his cattle, or for the safety of his family. He found himself on a road as often as an alpine meadow.

This morning, Gideon rode one of the Circle M saddle horses, thankfully not named by Malena and Rebecca, but who answered to the respectable handle of Copper. They had spent the morning checking pumps and culverts, and the few cattle and calves in the home pastures who had not been able to go up into the mountains during spring turnout. And on their return to the barn after lunch, Reuben had said, "Feel up to an errand this afternoon?"

With Seth and Reuben headed up the mountain to the main pump to figure out why the water pressure had dropped just enough to annoy Aendi Naomi and his cousins, Gideon and Copper had set out for Mountain Home to fetch some parts for a generator Reuben was rebuilding. He'd ridden about two miles when he saw a female figure in the distance, walking at such a rapid pace it was more of a forced march, head down and arms swinging.

Who could that be, out here in the hot sun and the wind, with nothing but miles of fenced pasture on either side? He nudged Copper into a trot, and soon caught up. Closer to, the set of her shoulders and the dark shape of her backpack purse told him the answer.

"Patricia?" he called as he narrowed the gap between them. "*Bischt du* okay? Did something happen?"

He drew even with her and slowed the horse, but she didn't stop. She dashed the tears off her face so hard with one hand it was almost a slap. "I'm fine. I'm going to work."

He knew she started her shift at the quilt shop at one o'clock. It was nearly two. "On foot?"

"I'm doing the best I can, Gideon Miller, and I'll thank you to keep your opinions to yourself."

Something must really have gone wrong. "Hold on, Patricia —stop."

"I can't stop. I'm already late."

"Let us give you a ride."

She slashed an incredulous glance sideways that was answer enough.

"I'm serious. This saddle is well worn in. It'll take two of us if you ride in front."

"I can't ride astride in a dress!"

"Hike it up a little. No one will see. Copper here will get you to town in no time."

With the tears already drying on her cheeks, he'd clearly made her an offer she couldn't refuse. He swung down and held the reins while she hoisted herself into the saddle, wriggled and fussed with her backpack, then adjusted her skirts until they came up almost to her knees and she could sit comfortably astride. He mounted behind her, and for the first time since he was a kid teaching Susanna how to ride, he gathered the reins into one hand and slid the other around a female waist.

It was not one bit like holding his sister.

"Hang onto the pommel and grip with your knees," he said. "I'm going to let Copper stretch his legs."

Copper was happy to oblige, though Gideon didn't let him gallop the entire way, of course. Alternating gaits, they covered the first mile, and then the second in far less time than he wanted to. As they slowed to a walk on the outskirts of town, he dared to let himself breathe in the scent of her warm skin and the shampoo she'd used in her hair. "I hope you don't think I'm taking advantage."

"How could you be?" she demanded breathlessly. "Goodness, this horse at a gallop is like riding in a truck with the windows down."

"Better," he replied. "He'll slow down when you want him to."

Her spine wilted against him, and it was all he could do not to gather her in closer. "You've heard."

"I haven't heard a thing. And you don't have to tell me if you don't want to."

"I don't. But I did something stupid, and now I might have to ask for your help."

"Don't sound so mad. I'm happy to help."

With a sigh, she straightened up, and got a better grip on the pommel. He wished she'd wrap her arms over his arm around her, but if he suggested it, he'd probably get a couple of elbows straight into his ribs for his trouble.

"Sunday night, on the bridge. I went to Idaho with Chance."

It was a lucky thing he had to keep her safely in the saddle, or he might have fallen off in shock. He knew Kate King had called the ranch Sunday night, but not the details. "Was it— Were you— Did he—"

"We went to a restaurant and I drank too much and my *Kapp* flew out the window and I threw up down the side of his truck."

Words were beyond him, so he gave in to instinct and simply pulled her against him in the best attempt at a sympathetic hug he could manage.

"He sent me flowers the next day."

"That was nice."

"They were awful. Gaudy. Struck my poor father speechless. And in the note Chance assured me the truck had not been damaged by the contents of my insides."

He couldn't help it. He tried not to laugh out loud, but his chest shook against her back. "A true gentleman." To his infinite relief, he caught the corner of a smile, too. "And that was all that happened? He didn't—take advantage?"

She shook her head, and the coil that had tightened in his stomach relaxed.

"But what I didn't expect was for him to turn up today in the cabin I was cleaning and offer me a ride to work just as if nothing had happened. He wouldn't take no for an answer. He followed me in the truck, all the way down that big long lane at the Rocking Diamond. And no Clara at the bottom. If I was going to be late for work at the quilt shop, I'd do it without his help, so I climbed their fake split-rail fence and started across the trail horses' pasture so he couldn't follow me. By the time I got to the field track, he'd figured out that I really meant it."

"He gave up?" She nodded. "What happened to Clara?"

"I don't know. Something must have. She always does what she says she's going to." The downtown part of Mountain Home came into view around the curve. "*Denki*, Gideon. I'm sorry to be so much *Druwwel*."

"You aren't any trouble at all. I'm fetching some parts for Reuben. Rose's is right on my way."

He turned Copper into the little parking lot across the highway, where Alden Stolzfus had built a roomy shed for the Amish horses visiting town. After Gideon dismounted, Patricia swung her leg over and slithered down into his arms.

For a single moment that would be engraved in his memory forever, he stood there with his arms looped around her waist, gazing down into those long-lashed, grey-green eyes that changed with her moods and endlessly fascinated him. How had he never noticed before that her eyes were level with his chin?

Her lashes dipped, and with a thrill that ran over him from head to foot, he realized her gaze had fallen to his mouth.

"Patricia!"

She practically came out of her skin. So did he, jumping back and releasing her.

Alden jogged out of the door of his shop. "I'm so glad you found her, Gideon." To Patricia, he said, "No one knew where you were. Water the horse, then you need to get get home right away."

"What happened?" she said on a gasp. "Mamm? Dat?"

"No, Aendi Annie."

"Ach, neh!" She wrapped both arms around her waist as though she'd gone cold.

"Your *mamm* went over to the *Daadi Haus* to take her something and found her unconscious in bed. She says she did wake up, but she won't let her get out of bed."

"Can you tell Rose—"

"Of course. When you didn't show up for work, she called Beth to come and help today anyway."

All she had to do was turn those eyes on Gideon, now filled with tears of sorrow, for him to reach for her. *"Kumm mit.* Copper and I will take you home." He led him over to the bucket so the horse could get a well-earned drink and a handful of oats.

"I called Zach when I saw you. He went over to your place," Alden said. "He can tell your parents you're on your way."

She nodded. *"Denki*, Alden. Call Simeon and Noah, too. They were working on the Cooper barn extension today. And Annie has two sons still living, both here in Montana. I'm sure Dat will have called them—he has their numbers in the little book he keeps in his pocket."

Alden nodded and jogged back into his shop.

When Copper had had enough to drink, she climbed back into the saddle more comfortably this time, probably because her mind had moved outward from her own problems to the elderly woman they all loved, and beyond her to prayer. After she settled her skirts, Gideon swung on behind her and this time, his arm held both steadiness and strength.

"Copper, gee," he said to the horse. "I know you're tired, but you can do it."

The *Englisch* might have taken an elderly family member to

the neurological clinic named for the Madisons' late eldest son on the other side of town, because it had a small emergency department in the rear. But the Amish knew that death was in the hands of *Gott*, and if He had determined that Annie's time had come, then no ambulance or hospital would change the course of events.

Copper was a horse made of more heart than muscle, it seemed. He must have recognized the tension in both their bodies, and was covering ground in such good time that they cleared the town limits in a few minutes. They began to see more buggies rolling down the highway than usual. The word was clearly out. A good portion were likely heading for the King place to do what they could to help.

When they reached the farm, Gideon knew better than to lift Patricia down, especially with her father already coming out of the door of the *Daadi Haus*. "Swing your leg over and I'll let you down slowly," he murmured. When her tennis shoes touched the dirt he swung down himself and slid the reins over Copper's head.

"People are on their way, Arlon. I'll take care of the horses," he said as Patricia fell into her father's hug. "Don't worry about a thing."

"*Denki*, Gideon," Patricia said over her shoulder as the two of them went into Annie's little home. "Again."

He had time for a smile before the door closed behind her.

He led Copper over to the rail, where he watered him again and secured him with enough slack that he could graze on the grass. The members of the *Gmay* wouldn't be here for a few minutes. Something compelled him into the little *Daadi Haus* to say a last good-bye to Annie if he could, even if it wasn't really his place.

Silently, he slid into the bedroom, staying out of the way.

He knew, of course, that at this moment he was the last thing Patricia would be thinking of. But still, if his presence could bring her comfort, he'd offer it gladly. He took up a post somewhere at the foot of the bed within arm's reach of her. She was standing with her father while Kate sat in a kitchen chair next to Annie, holding her hand. He'd heard that Annie Gingerich was past ninety, but she'd never really shown it other than needing support to walk distances greater than the width of her own kitchen. Her energy was all in her eyes, in her spirits, in her love of telling stories to the *Kinner* with different voices and energetic gestures. And every one of them true.

But now that energy, that crackling sense of life, had dimmed. She lay in her bed, her body hardly bigger than that of a child, eyes closed and breathing so shallowly her chest barely rose and fell. The Kings spoke quietly, talking about the comfort in the twenty-third Psalm when the Psalmist knew he was never alone in the valley of the shadow, and including her in the conversation, though she didn't respond.

Then Patricia told her where she'd been, and embroidered quite a fine tale about how she'd arrived at Annie's bedside "on horseback, Aendi, thanks to Gideon Miller."

And to Gideon's surprise, Annie's eyes opened. She looked confused about her surroundings for a moment, then seemed to relax as she recognized her own room and found her family's faces one by one. Her gaze moved from Patricia to Gideon—the faintest smile curved the corners of her lips—she locked eyes with Patricia again in an expression that he couldn't read.

It looked almost like ... approval.

And then her eyes widened, her frail old hand tightened on Kate's, and she looked past them all as though someone she loved were coming in the door whom she hadn't seen in a long while. And with a sigh, Annie, the oldest member of the

Siksika Valley *Gmay*, departed to take her place in the larger congregation singing around the throne of Heaven.

Gideon couldn't help himself. He slid one arm around Patricia, standing next to him, and pulled her into him in a hug. Silently, she buried her face in his chest. Her body shook with silent sobs, while her father murmured the Lord's prayer.

"Annie's body may have given out," Gideon whispered to Patricia when Arlon fell silent, holding his wife's hand. "But her heart was in *Gott*'s keeping, and that made it the strongest part of her."

Patricia still made no sound. But against his shirt, her head moved in a nod, with the conviction that he had spoken Annie's epitaph.

There was no need for any more words. He simply held Patricia until her grief quietened to sniffles, and handed her his wrinkled and sweat-stained hanky. While she blew her nose and went to comfort her mother, he bowed his head. Silently, he beseeched *der Herr* to welcome his beloved child Annie home, her frail body now laid aside and her loving heart rejoicing in the presence of the One she had longed to meet all her earthly life.

Her epitaph would never be carved into a headstone or painted in words for people to read. That was not the Amish way—a person's name and dates of birth and death were as far as it went. But it would be a living memory in the hearts of everyone in the *Gmay*, everyone who had known her, no matter how briefly.

Gideon could only hope that when his time came, his epitaph would be as true.

Later that evening

Patricia sat on the side of her bed, thankful for a moment of peace at last in which to deal with the day's shocks. They'd fallen like stones tossed in a pool, one after the other. Stones whose rings had no time to subside, colliding with one another and making a chaos all their own inside her. While Mamm and Dat quietly discussed funeral arrangements downstairs with the bishop and deacons, she tried to make sense of it all.

The fact was, Aendi Annie's death was the only thing that *did* make sense.

Gideon's coming to her rescue just in time to bring her back to Annie's bedside? That could only be the hand of *Gott*, seeing her home so that Annie to speak a farewell with her eyes.

And that glance? That smile of satisfaction—the one that held just a hint of *I told you so*? *Ach du Lieber*, could it really be that Annie's second-to-last thought on earth had been of her and Gideon?

That was either a miracle … or a disaster.

But somehow his strong arm around her waist, his unhesitating help and support—for goodness sake, his putting her first even before his own responsibilities—didn't feel disastrous. It felt … miraculous.

Gideon Miller. Of all people.

The man who had been as irritating as a burr in a sock, who had refused to be chased away by her grouchy behavior, had given her the gift of Annie's last moments. Annie's last wish, too, if that smile had been any indication—to see her and Gideon together.

Oh, Annie, you and your family legend of the wedding quilt. I never believed it for a minute. But I'm beginning to believe it now.

She'd never got the chance to ask for Gideon's help with the problem of Chance. To play pretend boyfriend until Chance got the message that he would never be anything more to her than an *Englisch* acquaintance. She couldn't ask Gideon to pretend. Not after this. In fact, she no longer wanted to pretend about anything.

All she wanted was to see him, talk to him, thank him for making those last moments possible. Then tell him ... what? *Old things are passed away; behold, all things are become new.* In the blink of an eye, everything had changed—heart, life, future. This was what it was like to grow up. To leave girlhood behind and become a woman.

One who was no longer interested in *Rumspringe.*

One whose heart belonged to *Gott*—and Gideon Miller.

One who wanted a future committed to both.

Hers had probably been the shortest *Rumspringe* ever in the valley—shorter even than Clara's. But if the purpose of that experience was to give a person what they needed to make a choice about the rest of their life, then she had had that in spades.

Patricia gazed at her lamplit reflection in the window, dark now with nightfall, and made up her mind.

Mei Vater, I choose the Amish life.

And I want to spend it with Gideon.

❧ 17 ❧

Thursday, August 18

ANNIE GINGERICH'S funeral was to be held on the third day after her death, according to Amish custom. On the day she died, while Noah and Simeon were building her simple casket, Kate had showed Patricia and Clara how to perform the last loving acts that an Amish woman could for one of their own. So, by sunset, clean and dressed in her usual widow's black, with the white organdy cape and apron in which she'd been married and carefully kept in her cedar chest all these years for just this purpose, Annie lay peacefully in her coffin on one of her own quilts.

The women of the west district, and some of Annie's friends in the east district, spent the first day cleaning both *Daadi Haus* and the main farmhouse from top to bottom. The men cleaned out the barn, both the horses' stalls and where the buggies were parked, then went upstairs to clean out the hay storage, the only space on the farm big enough to accommodate both congregations. Buggies went to the bus station to collect the relatives. Food flowed in, both for the family and for the day of the funeral.

Such was the care of the *Gmay* that the Kings and the two Gingerich sons and their families had little more to do than greet the stream of people who came for the viewing on Wednesday and Thursday, and sit down periodically to eat. Thursday evening the bench wagon arrived, and since the valley did not have two of them, people brought folding chairs if they had them. Clara and Patricia had already moved temporarily into the *Daadi Haus* so that Annie's sons and their wives could have their rooms, Simeon went to stay with the Bontragers, and Annie's grown grandchildren and their families stayed in the remaining rooms in the farmhouse.

Patricia had been involved in funerals before, of course— everyone in the *Gmay* had, even the little *Kinner*—but somehow it felt different with Aendi Annie. Annie had *seen* her in a way that few people did, and seemed to know her better than she knew herself. She'd made that discovery only at the last minute, and she was sorry now that she'd been so stubborn and wilful that she'd missed out on more opportunities to curl up next to her on the worn sofa and simply listen.

Tears welled in her eyes. But rather than weeping all over Clara, who had gone to bed early in order to be rested for tomorrow, Patricia took herself outside. Only a few buggies remained in the yard. She didn't really want to talk to anyone, so in the golden hour she ambled off down the track between the two home pastures where she'd walked with her brother Noah what seemed like years ago. Wildflowers waved in the breeze, catching the last of the light in their petals and limning them with gold. Daisies, yarrow, dill, and bachelor's buttons brushed her skirts, and the scent of hay filled her senses. They'd be taking off the second crop soon.

She glanced at the sky to the north, where clouds were piling up on the peaks like whipped cream on oatmeal topping. *Please don't rain and be horrible tomorrow.* But it would be appropriate to see the very sky mourning Annie.

"Patricia?"

His voice sent a *zing!* from heart to toes and fingertips. She turned with a smile to see Gideon wading through the wildflowers that had overgrown the track.

"I wasn't sure you'd want company," he said as he joined her, "if you were taking a walk to get some alone time."

"I don't want most company," she agreed, "but that doesn't include you." Before he could respond, she said, "I want to thank you, Gideon, for everything you did on Tuesday. Especially getting me home in time to see Aendi Annie before she went. That meant a lot to me. So did your comfort. That was really the help of a friend."

His cornflower blue eyes studied hers. "I'm glad you see me as a friend. You didn't always."

"I know, and I'm sorry for it." Her lashes fell. "For a lot of other things, too. You'll be happy to know my *Rumspringe* is over."

"Did it even last a week?"

"Barely. But this week ... I've grown up. Realized what the important things are. I'm going to talk to the bishop about baptism classes this fall."

One hand moved, as though he wanted to reach for her, then thought better of it. She mourned the tiny loss, but didn't dare take his hand. Not yet.

"I'm glad," was all he said. "Have you told your parents?"

She shook her head. "I'll tell them Sunday. After everything is over."

"It will be *gut* for them to have joyful news along with the sad," he said. "I'm happy you told me. Really happy."

She met his gaze again, and saw something in it that gave her courage. "Are you?"

He took a breath, as though he'd made a decision. "It means that I can court you. If you'd like that."

Here was the moment—the point of no return—and she took it with a canter. "I would," she said softly. "I know we haven't always gotten along, but..."

"But it feels different now." He took a step closer, and turned to fold his arms on top of the fence. She did the same, but let her bare elbow touch his below the rolled-up shirtsleeve.

Somehow it felt as intimate as a kiss.

"That night," he said, his voice a little husky, "Annie looked at the two of us and then smiled. What was that about?"

The two of us. Could any words be more thrilling?

"Remember when I told you about the family tradition? The wedding quilt?"

"You said you'd started *a* quilt. But you laughed about the tradition."

"I'm not laughing now. Annie was convinced that since I met you in February and started the quilt in August, you and I were—" She stopped. *Too soon.* "Anyway, she thought a lot of you."

"So she was giving us her approval?"

A blush was already creeping up Patricia's neck. "Only Annie knows for sure, but ... it looked that way to me. With a side of *I told you so.*"

He laughed—a real laugh, with his whole body. He slapped the rail with his other hand. "I love that woman. In her last moments, too." The humor faded from his face. "What a privilege—to be in her final thoughts like that. How generous she was."

"That's what I've just been thinking. Do you know what she said about you a few days ago?" She flicked a glance at him. "Don't go getting a swelled head, but she said, *Gideon Miller is the solution to this whole problem.* Little did she know."

He peered into her face. "What whole problem?"

With a wave of her other hand—she was not moving her elbow from his for anything—she said, "Oh, you know. Chance Madison. Annie thought that if he saw you with me more, he'd leave me alone."

"Well, I'm a hundred percent behind that idea."

"Then, it would have been pretend," she said softly. "Now ... I want it to be real. Not because I need protecting, but because I want to do things together. Having ice cream on the nights I work late. Walking in this meadow. Silly things like that."

His expression had gone from grim to slowly dawning delight. "You mean it?"

"I do."

Now he lifted her arm and tucked it into the crook of his elbow, there on the fence. It felt inevitable that she would wrap her hand around his bare forearm, deeply tanned and as warm as a glowing fire in the deepening cool of the evening.

"I am a happy man," he proclaimed to the neighboring hay field. "Patricia and I are courting."

She had to laugh. "Lucky for you they can't hear us at the house. My cousins would never let us hear the end of it."

"I'm not afraid. But the person who should really hear about it is Chance Madison."

She thought so, too. "Maybe I'll tell Zefra. The word will get to him. If he knows we've had a death in the family, it will only be courteous to stay away."

"Don't be so certain. The Madisons buy hay from your dad, don't they?"

"*Ja*, but they're certainly not close friends. I can't see them wanting to pay their respects to a woman they probably didn't even know."

"They might want to pay their respects to the living, not the dead."

"I don't want to talk about them. I don't want to waste what time we have." She shook her head. "Tomorrow, after the service, I'll be eating lunch with the family, so I might not get much of a chance to talk with you."

"But you'll know I'm there," he said softly. He turned, and somehow his arms found their way around her waist. Hers looped around his neck as though they had no other place to be. "Every minute. Praying for you and your family, and sending you strength."

Her mouth trembled. "*Denki.*"

She thought he might kiss her, but the moment was too solemn despite all the beauty around them. Instead, he took off his straw hat and leaned his forehead against hers.

"I want to kiss you. But I won't. Not until all this is past."

She nodded. "Just so you know, I'll be waiting."

And when he laughed and drew back, it didn't feel like a loss. Especially when he slid his callused fingers through hers and they turned back onto the track. And two people who had come separately in the golden hour walked slowly home in the twilight, hands entwined and hearts marveling at how quickly and completely the road ahead had changed.

Friday, August 19

The funeral service was to start at nine, and by eight-thirty, the home fields held neat rows of buggies with the horses still hitched up, the boys acting as hostlers to keep things orderly. When Gideon took his place with the single men toward the back of the hay floor, he found Patricia not on the other side with the single women, but up at the front in the two rows reserved for the family. Annie's coffin rested on sawhorses between the men's and women's sections.

He'd heard that at *Englisch* funerals, there were masses of flowers and an organ playing and ushers guiding people into their seats. But in the Amish church, everyone knew their place, so an usher wasn't needed. Only two hymns would be sung—one at the end and one by the family at the graveside later. And all the flowers remained outside in the garden where Annie and Kate had planted them.

Annie's spirit was with *Gott*. She longer needed her frail earthly body, so it would go back to the earth from which man had been created. The *Gmay* would celebrate the One who had made her salvation possible, not the one who had departed their number.

Gideon had been taught that a person lived not for this life, but for the one to come. But this morning, as the *Gmay* fell silent and Paul Petersheim, one of the ministers from the east district, rose to begin, he had to admit that this life was turning out to be pretty sweet. He could still hardly believe that for all the time it had taken him to work up the courage to approach Patricia in the fields last night, her response had been so decided and so immediate that it almost seemed as though it couldn't have happened. That he must have dreamed it.

But it was true. She might be in the front and he might be with Seth away in the back of a congregation that was twice as big as usual. But the very fact that they were here together—and together in spirit—was enough for him.

The funeral service was about an hour and a half, much shorter than a regular church service. It began, not with a sung hymn, but with one read by the minister. He and the preacher from the west district followed with several passages from scripture, beginning with the fathers of old, Elijah, and ending with Hebrews.

These all died in faith, not having received the promises, but having seen them afar off, and were persuaded of them, and embraced them, and confessed that they were strangers and pilgrims on the earth.

Paul's sermon was short and heartfelt—the Petersheim family had lived in the Siksika almost as long as the Gingeriches.

The bishop rose, and after reading a prayer from the *Christenpflicht*, he read the obituary that Kate and Annie's sons had written. Gideon had a feeling that his sermon was a reflection of Annie's convictions about the transitory nature of death and the eternal solidity of salvation, probably gleaned in many conversations with her over the years. It made him glad for the little gifts that made life sweet along the path, with that great promise waiting at the end that no man could take away.

The service concluded with many a furtive swipe at the eyes, and even Gideon's voice trembled in the beginning when they sang *Lied* number 136, the final hymn, together.

Muß es nun seyn gescheiden
So woll uns Gott begleiten,

Ein jedes an fein Ort;
Da wollend Fleiß ansehren,
Unf'r Leben zu bewähren
Nach Inhalt Gottes Wort.

If we must now be parted,
Then may our God with us depart,
Each of us to his own place;
There we with diligence will move,
And by our lives will seek to prove,
The precepts of God's Word with grace.

After filing past the coffin for the final viewing of Annie's calm face, it was almost a shock to the system to go back down the stairs with his brother to the barn and ordinary life.

"Want company for the walk?" Seth asked.

Gideon nodded. "The cemetery isn't far. Half a mile, maybe." He glanced up at a sky nearly filled with lowering clouds. "Do you think Little Joe shortened things up some so that the burial could happen before it rains?"

"No telling. But I hope any rain we get is short and sweet and doesn't spoil the hay."

That was up to *Gott*, and they both knew it.

When they reached the Amish graveyard, Gideon realized that of all the times he'd passed it, he'd never yet been through the gate. Annie's was the first funeral he'd been to since their family had moved here. The hearse drawn by two horses led the procession, and dozens of buggies made an orderly black line for almost a mile, each turning in and finding the grassy margins where they were neatly lined up, again by the boys assigned to help. Annie's coffin was carried to her grave, then quietly placed on ropes held by those who had dug it by hand.

The family gathered round, the *Gmay* in a rustling silence broken only by the occasional murmur or high voice of a *Kind*.

Instead of the bishop's reading the graveside hymn, the *Vorsinger* lifted up his voice and the *Gmay* joined him in a hymn Gideon had sung at many funerals—*Lied* number 125, which they traditionally started at verse 57.

> Es sind zween Weg in dieser Zeit,
> Der ein ist schmal, die andern weit
> Wer jetzt will gehn die schmale Bahn,
> Der wird veracht von jedermann.

> *There are two ways in this our time*
> *The one is narrow, the other wide*
> *Who now will take the narrow way,*
> *He is despised on every side.*

The verse began with a person's feet firmly on the earth, but the final verse made it clear that their journey had only one destination.

> Stred sich zum vergestedten Ziel
> Dann wer das Kleinod g'winnen will,
> Muß alls verlagn, aus diser Bahn,
> Will er erlangen diese Kron.

> *Press on toward the hidden goal*
> *Then he who makes the prize his own*
> *Must forsake all highways but this path,*
> *If he wants to obtain this crown.*

Gideon would have given anything to be able to stand at

Patricia's side as the coffin was lowered and the Amish undertakers picked up their shovels. But she was surrounded by her family and the Gingeriches, and it wouldn't have been fitting. This was no time for the urgings of human feelings. This was the time to mourn, and to contemplate the higher of the two ways. He knew that. And yet...

"Kumm mit, Bruder." Susanna and Stephen materialized at his side and somehow he was walking away with them and Seth instead of toward Patricia. Just as well. At least he would see her back at the farm.

Instead of squeezing her two brothers into the buggy with herself, Stephen, and Mamm and Luke, Susanna and her intended joined him and Seth for the walk back to the King place. "I know we see you often," she said, "but it's not often enough. I hear you rescued Patricia on the road and got her home in time to say her farewells."

"I think *Gott* did the rescuing," he admitted. "I was just the guy he used. And Copper, of course. That horse has more endurance than any of us. And willingness."

"He probably wasn't distracted by a certain someone," Seth put in for no reason at all.

"I don't know what you're talking about." Gideon might be ready to stand at Patricia's side, but he was *not* ready to be teased about her by his family.

"We'll let it go for now," Susanna told him, "because it's a solemn day. But I saw you riding double with that certain someone from the upstairs window at the Inn when I was changing beds. You can't fool me."

But they couldn't know what had happened during Annie's last moments. Or in the sunset last night. All his siblings knew was that he and Patricia didn't get along. "Only because she had no other choice."

And then buggies began to clatter past them and they had to change to the other side of the road or hold up the returning procession.

When they emerged into the yard from the King lane, a dozen helpers, including Aendi Naomi and her daughters and daughters-in-law, present and future, who had stayed behind from the cemetery, had set up the benches out on the lawn under the trees and loaded a row of folding tables with food. Since a death couldn't exactly be predicted or planned for in most cases, there hadn't been the months of preparation that would have been necessary for a wedding. Every family had brought what they had on hand, which was more than enough to feed the entire congregation. They took plates cafeteria style and the tables filled as the hostlers unhitched the horses and put the buggies in neat rows in the pasture.

Gideon's brother Tobias's wedding to Sylvia, which had barely a couple of weeks' notice, might wind up being pot luck too. Not that the bridal couple would mind. But it was coming up very soon and he could already imagine the lists his mother and Sylvia were making.

He could feel the moment the King family climbed out of their buggy some time later, and glanced over his shoulder from his place at the table to meet Patricia's gaze from all the way across the yard. He couldn't keep the smile off his face, and was rewarded by a tired smile in return before her attention was claimed by her mother. A section of tables had been saved for them, and plates were pressed into the family's hands as the buffet line opened to make way for them.

The rest of the afternoon, Gideon couldn't get close enough to Patricia to speak. But he was always aware of her— leaning her head on Clara's black-clad shoulder, taking one of her little cousins into the house to the bathroom, speaking soberly with Naomi and Rebecca over by the vegetable garden. The family needed this time with the *Gmay* to mourn, to remember, to re-tell some of Annie's stories to the *Kinner*, just as she would have done.

And once again, just being near enough to exchange a glance with her—to let her know he was there for her—was enough.

❧ 18 ❧

Saturday, August 20

YESTERDAY THE *GUT Gott* had held back the rain until evening, after everyone had gone and Patricia's exhausted family and the Gingeriches were content to collapse in the nearest chair and fill the farmhouse with stories and memories of Aendi Annie. This morning it was still raining, the clouds filling the skies in the bowl of the mountains. Dat was happy about it, though. He hadn't planned to cut the hay for another week at least, so the rain would give it a last boost of moisture that would only make it more nutritious for the cattle come winter.

Even as she did her morning chores, Patricia's mind kept wandering to Gideon and the chores he might be doing on the Circle M today. He wouldn't be riding up on the allotments, that was certain. Not because of the weather, but because of church tomorrow. She and Clara had already cleaned the house, but it would take Dat and a few of the neighbors a few days to move the hay bales from the first cutting back into the loft. Annie's sons had offered to stay to help him, but Dat knew as well as any of them that they had their own farms and animals to take care of, so this morning after breakfast they had all piled into a couple of *Englisch* taxis for the trip back to the bus station and home.

That left her and Clara with the utter luxury of working on their quilts after lunch. Her wedding quilt. For Patricia in her most private thoughts saw this quilt lying on their bed to keep her and Gideon warm after they were married. Was it tempting fate to think that way? Some people might feel it was, but she didn't. She was simply acknowledging that *Gott*'s hand had brought her together with the one man meant for her. She couldn't wait to come to know him better and better during their courtship. And to spend each day for the rest of her life being grateful for *Gott*'s care of them.

She didn't know when a wedding would happen, or what experiences they might have to work through before that, but she was willing for every step that took her closer to the day when she could stand in front of the congregation with him and say "I will."

In the meantime, she had to finish making up these nine-patches so that they would frame the blocks that she now couldn't help but think of as Bear Claws. When she was done, she wouldn't waste another minute before walking over to the bishop's to talk to him about baptism classes. And after their talk, would it be too forward to call on the folks at the Circle M in hopes that Gideon might have come in from work?

What a *wunderbaar* day it might yet turn out to be!

By midafternoon all the nine-patches were made and neatly stacked to wait for the next step. Patricia left Clara happily humming "How Great Thou Art" behind her sewing machine as she pumped the treadle in time. She resisted the urge to tease her sister about what was making her so happy on a grey and gloomy day. But she did wonder if Calvin, with his usual complete unawareness of the appropriate or the solemn, might have asked Clara at the funeral yesterday if he could give her a ride home from singing after church tomorrow.

No, she wouldn't tease. Especially when Patricia hadn't yet told her family of the unexpected fork in her own life's path.

"Mamm, I'm going over to see the Wengerds," she said to her mother as she walked into the kitchen.

"In this weather?" Mamm was sorting the baked goods left over from yesterday for the inevitable visitors tomorrow—coconut chocolate chip cookies, regular chocolate chip cookies, jam tarts, sand tarts, and what smelled like a carrot cake, rich with cream cheese frosting.

"It's not so bad now." Patricia glanced out the window over the sink. "I think it's slacking off."

"Put on your boots, and take an umbrella."

Patricia took half the advice. Who wore gumboots in August? It was just a summer storm, not spring breakup. So she put on the pair of canvas tennis shoes that didn't have the hole in the toe and found the little folding umbrella on the top shelf of the closet. She didn't exactly want to show up at the bishop's house—or the Circle M—looking like she'd fallen in the river. At the last minute, she pulled a black knitted cardigan off the coat hook and slipped it on over her black dress, cape, and apron, then set out.

At the end of their road, which intersected with the county highway, she turned left at the schoolhouse. From behind it came the regular *thunk!* of someone splitting wood, probably for the stove in the schoolhouse. She hoped it wasn't the bishop, who owned the property but had ceded it to the school in perpetuity. She had about half a mile to go when she heard the rumble of a big engine making the turn out of the Rocking Diamond's gates.

She knew that sound.

Sure enough, Chance Madison slowed and rolled at a walking pace beside her. The passenger window slid down and she couldn't help it—she ran a fast glance over the whole door to check that no, the contents of her insides had inflicted no damage on its glossy cherry-red surface.

"Hey, Patty. Can I give you a ride somewhere?"

No matter how many times she told him how she preferred to be called, he ignored it. He must have a mental block. She shook her head. "No, thanks. I'm just going to Wengerds'. I'm almost there."

"It's half a mile. Let me give you a lift to the driveway."

"Honest, Chance. I'm fine."

"Patty, just let me do this for you. I'm still feeling bad about the trip to Idaho. And—oh—" A thought seemed to strike him as he took in her all-black clothes. "I'm sorry about your aunt."

"Great-aunt. Thank you. As for the other, you sent flowers." They were impossible, but— "It was kind of you and I appreciate the thought."

"I'm still sorry, though. Please? You may not have noticed, but it's raining."

The rain was, in fact, not slacking off at all. The clouds seemed to be renewing their onslaught on the thirsty fields.

"Oh, all right. Just to their lane, though. Little Joe probably wouldn't appreciate this ginormous truck clogging up his yard if they're expecting company."

Chance seemed to take this as a compliment. He was

smiling as he pushed the door open for her. She tried to be equally courteous, shaking out the umbrella before she climbed in.

As she snapped the seatbelt into place, he said, "You look nice, even if you have mud on your shoes."

"Do I?" She peered down. "Did I track mud into your clean truck?"

He laughed. "You're like that cartoon character, making a mess wherever he goes. But you're still cute."

"Oh, ha ha." She blinked as they shot past the bishop's lane at twice the speed of a horse going flat out. "Hey! You missed the driveway. It was that one on the left we just passed."

"I know. But you can visit Joe Wengerd anytime. Like tomorrow. You have church, right?"

"Well, yes, but—" She took a deep breath and tried not to screech at the big lug. "The point is, I have something important to talk to him about, and he'll be busy tomorrow doing bishop things." When he only nodded, she said a little more firmly, "Chance, turn around. Please."

"I will. I promise. But I hear the weather in Libby is clear and sunny. Maybe we could go to a movie. You'd think this podunk town—"

Which they were passing through at this moment. Patricia lowered the window and prayed that someone she knew would be outside. She needed to call in reinforcements.

"—would have a movie theater, wouldn't you? But no. The closest thing they have is a video arcade, and I maxed them all out before I was twelve."

Why wasn't anyone on the sidewalk? It was only a little rain.

They flew past Rose Garden Quilts, whose door was closed but whose OPEN—PLEASE WALK IN sign hung on the front.

The feed store? *Ach, denkes, mein Gott.* She leaned out the window—hanging on to her *Kapp* this time—and waved her folded-up umbrella at Tobias Miller, who had stopped his buggy in the yard exit to wait for them to pass. She had a split-second view of his puzzled and slightly disapproving face before they were past and over the bridge into the residential part of town.

Oh, help me. He thinks I'm on Rumspringe. He thinks I'm going willingly.

But did that mean he would keep quiet about it or tell someone? She needed him to say he'd seen her.

"Chance, for heaven's sake, I don't want to go to Libby or anywhere else! Let me out. I'll walk back to the bishop's."

"Naw, you don't want to do that."

"Don't tell me what I want!" She lost her temper and did the exact opposite of what the Bible said. *A soft answer turneth away wrath.* "What I want is to talk to the bishop about getting baptized! Stop this truck at once or—or I'll—"

"Jump out?"

They were out of town to the first big curve where the highway turned south toward Libby. "Chance!" She yanked her arm inside and folded both arms over her chest, one hand still holding the wet umbrella in a death grip, doing her level best not to use it on his head.

"Come on, Patty, where's your sense of fun? I'm just trying to show you a good time. You liked it before, didn't you?"

"Did you hear what I just said?"

"*Stop this truck at once.*" He mimicked her tone and her *Deitsch* accent perfectly.

"Before that."

"*What I want is to talk to the bishop about getting baptized.*"

How eerie that he could do that. "Does that mean you won't be riding with me anymore?"

"That's exactly what it means," she snapped. "Or working for your mother, or having anything to do with you or other worldly people."

"Oh, I don't think that would be a good idea." And before she could get the breath back his words had just knocked out of her, he went on, "I know you don't mean it. You're just running scared from me, after what happened in Idaho. But I promise I've learned my lesson. You'll see."

"If you had, you'd do as I ask and take me back." Her teeth were beginning to chatter. But not from cold. They were nearly ten miles out of town now. She couldn't see the speedometer, but she was pretty sure it was standing well over the 55 MPH posted on the speed limit sign.

But he didn't seem to hear. "After we spend the rest of the weekend getting to know each other better, you'll see how good we are together." He glanced at her, and his expression softened into a smile. "I guess it's pretty obvious I'm in love with you."

You're insane, is what you are.

"Where ... are we going?"

He seemed to take this as encouragement. "If you don't want to go to Libby, we have a hunting cabin about forty miles east, just before the park. It's right on a lake. Me and my brothers go there with friends even when we aren't hunting. Dad keeps it fully stocked—and I mean *fully*. Condoms and everything."

Condoms. The word echoed like a dinner gong in her brain, sounding stranger with each repetition. She'd seen those in the drugstore. The Amish didn't use birth control of any kind, because *Kinner* were a blessing only *Gott* could bestow in His perfect time. When it was His time for a couple to have one *Boppli*, or another *Boppli*, going against His will and preventing it was a sin.

And then it hit her exactly what he meant.

"I have no intention of—of doing anything like that," she said on a gasp.

"Like what?"

"Anything that requires the use of condoms."

"Ever?"

"Not until I'm married."

He smiled, as though she'd said exactly the right thing. "Then I guess we'll just have to get married."

She stared at him while every sensible word flew out of her head in fright.

Say something. Convince him somehow. Now.

"Chance, I can't marry you. I'm Amish."

"Don't you have to be baptized first to be really Amish?"

"I am really Amish," she said with slow emphasis. "Born, raised, and living Amish."

"But you're not baptized yet. You have to be before you can get married." He glanced at her. "I did my research. I wanted to know everything about you. There are a lot of YouTube videos out there about Amish stuff, did you know that? So we *can* get married, as long as you're not baptized."

"Chance, listen to me. I mean it." She almost reached over to touch his arm, then thought better of it. "I can't marry you. There's someone else. We're planning to marry." *Forgive me, Gideon, for this little fib. Even though it's true on my side.* "I'm even making my wedding quilt."

He didn't reply, just kept his eyes on the highway as the mountains slowly gave way to the foothills. Then he said, "But once we get to the cabin, you might change your mind. You might find out you like me better than him. Then you could make your quilt for me instead. I'd like that. I've never had a quilt, never mind a wedding quilt. Mom doesn't like them. Says they're too old-fashioned."

"Chance—"

"Look, here's the turn already." He smiled at her. "You make time fly, Patty."

He slowed to make the turn where the highway sign said Kootenai Peak State Park and pointed left. For one mad second she thought about jumping out, but she'd probably break her legs and even if she didn't, he'd only follow her in the truck for forty miles until she collapsed.

Her cold hand clutched the umbrella, her fingers stiffened around it from fear. Her cardigan was damp where she'd been hugging herself.

The umbrella.

As he swung the truck to the left, she hung her arm casually out the window. "Chance! Look out!"

"What?" He gripped the wheel, peering through the windshield to scan the road, the sky, the wet meadows for danger.

She dropped the umbrella. Under the engine's growl, she didn't even hear it land.

"I thought it was a bird flying at us, but it was only a piece of garbage."

"I didn't see anything."

"My fault. Sorry." She crossed her arms again.

A black folding umbrella. It could belong to anyone. Lots of people had them. But if anyone came looking for her, at least it was something out of place, to show they'd made that turn.

And if they made another one, she still had her cardigan. And her *Kapp*.

Protect me, Father. Keep me in the hollow of your hand. Give me the cunning of a fox, the soothing voice of a dove, and if it comes to it, the speed of a pronghorn antelope. Send help, O Lord, in my time of need. Give them perception to see that umbrella, and understanding to know what it means. Let me trust fully in Your protection, Lord.

O Lord of hosts, blessed is the man that trusteth in Thee.

❦ 19 ❦

THE CIRCLE M RANCH

GIDEON FINISHED his chores early on purpose—Seth was still mucking out the horse stalls, while Gideon had already finished the calving pens, a job almost as onerous. This was the second time this week, because church was at the Circle M tomorrow and everything had to be spotless. But hurrying work gave him an hour of spare time to spend on something increasingly valuable to him—as long as Onkel Reuben didn't turn up with a few more suggestions.

He hitched up Hammie, the black buggy horse that Reuben and Naomi had silently made available for him, and was sliding the big barn door open when Zach appeared just outside. He'd got off shift earlier and had changed from the Amish shirt made up in a color that matched the uniforms of the EMTs into a regular one.

"Heading out? Mind if I hitch a ride over to Wengerds'?"

"You can probably beat me over there if you take the shortcut."

Zach grinned. "But then I'd be soaking wet and probably muddy, and Ruby wouldn't let me in the door."

There was something to be said for that argument, he had to admit. "Hop in."

He took Zach all the way down to the house, then, even though the minutes were ticking past, it was only polite to say hello to the bishop and his family. He'd be quick. But two minutes turned into fifteen and a big piece of date nut cake before he could say his farewells and climb into the the buggy again.

"Let's go over to Patricia's, Hammie." Vulcan's Hammer was a retired racehorse, and new to the Circle M, but Reuben wasn't keen on naming things after worldly gods, so he'd become Hammie. He was smart and fast even yet, so it wasn't long before they were crunching up the King lane and coming to a stop under a spreading tree that would keep Hammie relatively dry.

Then he loped up the steps to find Kate waiting at the door. "Why, Gideon," she said in welcome. "Orlan is out in the barn with the hay crew, if you need him."

Color burned into his cheeks. "Um, actually, I wondered if Patricia was home."

For a moment she just gazed at him—he saw the moment the penny dropped—and she smiled and opened the door wider. "I'm afraid she's run over to the bishop's. I don't think she'll be long—do you want to come in and wait? I have any number of baked goods that people have been kind enough to bring."

"To the bishop's?" he repeated. "Are you sure?"

"Yes, she left about half an hour ago."

"Well, I just came from there and she wasn't with them."

"Maybe she was in the back with Ruby?"

"Zach was with me, and Ruby was in the kitchen when we got there. Are you sure?"

"That's where she said she was going. Unless—no, she wouldn't do that."

He waited, but Kate only looked down and fussed with the cling wrap on a tray of snickerdoodles.

"She wouldn't have done that, Kate," he said at last, reading her unhappy face. "Said she was going to Wengerds' and then gone somewhere else. Her *Rumspringe* is over. She was going to talk to him about taking baptism classes."

Kate's eyes filled with tears, but her face lit up with joy.

Behind him, Clara came into the kitchen. "Who's taking baptism classes?"

"Your sister," Kate finally managed. "Apparently." Her eyes shone. "Why didn't she talk to us about it? And how do you know this?" she said to Gideon.

"I'm sure she'll tell you when she gets home." His shirt collar was undone two buttons, but somehow it still felt constricting. Then something occurred to him. "She might have taken a shortcut across the fields. I didn't see her on the road after I left Wengerds'."

"The only shortcut between their place and ours has a pasture with a big bull in it," Clara pointed out. "No one ever goes that way. It's shorter to go around by the schoolhouse."

At a loss, Gideon wondered what he should do next. Had he somehow missed a slender figure in black walking in the rain?

No. Impossible. He'd never miss *her* slender figure, no matter what the weather was doing.

Boots sounded on the stairs—*thumpthumpthump*—and Arlon King pushed open the kitchen door. He was holding a cell phone like a rock he wanted to throw, and hay clung to his shirt and pants. Had a call interrupted his work?

"*Fraa*, didn't Patricia go over to the bishop's?"

"*Ja*, I thought so," Kate said. "But Gideon here tells me she wasn't there. Why? Arlon, has something happened?"

"Well, I don't know." Arlon blinked at Gideon, clearly unaware until that second that he'd even been in the room. "I guess she wasn't. That was Tobias Miller." He waggled the old black cell phone. "He just got back to the Inn and called to tell me that he saw our *Dochder* riding in Chance Madison's truck. They passed him at the feed store heading through town, going the opposite direction from home."

The bottom dropped out of Gideon's stomach. Riding in that man's truck? After all that had passed between them last evening? After all the hopes and dreams that had been born in his heart, all the sweet plans that had kept him awake half the night?

Had it all been a sham? A fake? An act to keep him from guessing the real truth—that her *Rumspringe* wasn't over at all, but in fact was about to get seriously wild?

With Chance Madison. Who apparently only had to stop the truck for her to throw the future into the ditch and hop in.

He thought he might be sick.

"This doesn't make sense," Clara said into a room that practically rang with silent confusion. "She was going over to talk to the bishop about baptism classes and suddenly she's going somewhere with Chance Madison?"

"She was what?" Arlon's eyes practically fell out of his head. "Baptism classes? Who told you that?"

Clara tilted her head at Gideon.

"I was so happy," Kate whispered. "But I don't understand."

Though the blood pounded in his ears, Gideon nodded to answer Arlon's question. Then he shrugged. "She told me last night she was going to. I don't know what possessed— Why she would—" He couldn't go on.

"Dat, did Tobias say anything else?" Clara asked.

"Only that she waved at him with her umbrella. And that she looked worried. Not like a person joyriding or having fun."

Worried. What did that mean? Gideon tried to imagine it. Would she be worried that Tobias had seen her and would tell on her? Or was something else going on that he couldn't quite grasp?

"She did take an umbrella," Kate said, clearly relieved that here was one fact that could be proved. "When she left the house. And that old black cardigan." She waved at the coat tree.

And then a terrible thought flared in Gideon's head like a struck match. "He did that once before," he said suddenly. "Offered her a ride and then took her all the way to Idaho. What if—" His throat closed. It was crazy. They would think he was nuts. Or so jealous of his rival that he'd say anything just to make him look bad. But he couldn't keep the words in. "What if he did it again?" he finished hoarsely.

"That would explain why she looked worried," Clara said. "Or angry. Or scared. And had the window down on a rainy day. So she could call to someone if she got the chance."

Kate clutched her husband's arm. "If she's not on *Rumspringe* and he's taking her somewhere against her will —Arlon—"

And suddenly Gideon knew what he had to do. It had been staring him in the face and he'd been too betrayed and angry to see it. "I've got the buggy. I'll go after her. They might still be in town. He might have taken her to a bar or something. Like he did before."

But Clara was already shaking her head. "There's only one bar in Mountain Home, and they'd already passed it if Tobias saw them go by the feed store. If he was going as fast as Tobias said, it wasn't to the library. Or the sports complex. He was making time through town and heading south."

Libby. Or farther. *Please, lieber Gott, no.* "At the speed that truck can make, they could be in Whitefish by suppertime."

The buggy couldn't compete with that. But he knew of someone who could give it a run for its money.

"Call Jimmy," he said to Arlon. "Hire him to take me and Clara to Libby. That truck sticks out like a sore thumb, and you can hear it long before you can see it. If he's taken her there, we'll find her."

Clara was already running upstairs. She returned before Arlon had even reached Jimmy, the *Englisch* taxi driver, a warm jacket over her arm and her sturdy work shoes on. "Mamm, I don't know when we'll be back. But we should take something to eat with us. Patricia might be hungry."

There was no shortage of something to eat in the kitchen of an Amish family the day after a funeral. By the time Arlon concluded his call, Clara had ready-made sandwiches, cake, cookies, a small round of the Zook brothers' Brie cheese, fruit, and four bottles of water stuffed into her backpack purse, which she slung over one shoulder by its strap.

"Your mother and I should go," Arlon said unhappily. "I don't like this plan at all."

Clara didn't even blink. "Patricia said Aendi Annie said something to her before she took sick. She said that if a person needed a nice-sized man between herself and someone she wanted to get rid of, Gideon would be the man she'd choose."

Gideon's mouth fell open in astonishment, but he had the wits to seize his moment. "If there was ever a time to heed Annie's advice, Arlon, it's now. Clara and I will go. You and

Kate keep the phone close. We'll use Jimmy's phone to call you when we know something."

"And get the phone trees working among the *Gmay*," Clara added. "If they haven't left town after all, maybe someone else has seen her."

Gideon had never really noticed Clara before, except as Patricia's sister. He'd never had an opportunity to appreciate this girl's cool head in a crisis. She would make an excellent EMT.

Denki, mei Vater, for Clara, he said to *der Herr* as Jimmy's white van with the big V8 engine rocked to a stop in the yard. *Be with us now, and help us to find Patricia safe. Lead us to her, Lord, and—and please let me hold her in my arms again.*

And this time, I won't let go.

I STILL HAVE MY CARDIGAN. I STILL HAVE MY KAPP. I HAVE MY cape and apron. And if worse comes to worst, I have hairpins.

Patricia wasn't quite sure what she'd do with nine metal hairpins, but she'd read in a book once that you could pick a lock with them.

The rain was beginning to move off to the south, and behind them the clouds lifted enough to send a wash of watery light over the narrow two-lane road. The shadow of the truck stretched out ahead of them for a moment before they rounded a curve and the shoulder of the hill blocked the last light.

"How much farther?" she asked. "I have to use the restroom."

"Not far. Just a few more miles. So you can't wear your hair down? You always have to wear that cap?"

They'd been talking about Amish customs for twenty miles. Talking about hat brims and horses was better by far than mentioning condoms or marriage again, so she did her best to keep her tone friendly and yet allow her convictions to shine through.

"The covering means something, though," she told him. "Scripture says that a woman should cover her head when she prays. Well, since a person never knows when they might pray at any minute of the day, it makes sense to simply have the covering on all the time, to be ready when the need strikes."

"You don't seriously pray all day long." He sounded skeptical.

"Not all day. But anytime. If my sister aggravates me, I pray for patience. If I'm out in the garden and I see something is getting ripe, I give thanks for it. If one of my friends is sick, I pray she'll get better."

"That's a lot of praying."

"It's kind of an ongoing thing," she agreed.

"So when you go swimming, you still wear the cap?"

"I haven't been swimming in a long time—the river is freezing. I'm not my brothers, that's for sure. But if I did, I'd tie on a headscarf. We call those a *Duchly*. This covering was made by my mother." She touched the white brim that covered her ear. "She wouldn't be very impressed if I wore it in the water and got it stained. Plus, all the starch would come out and it would look very sad and wilted."

"What happened to the one you lost out the window? That was all messed up?"

She'd wanted to throw it away. "Mamm washed it with her special detergent and got it clean again. A bit of starch and it was good as new." She paused. "I only have three, so it was a big deal to lose one. I'm glad you found it."

"I am, too, in that case. I thought you'd have one for every day of the week."

How many miles had it been? Was he slowing down?

She began to wriggle out of the cardigan.

"Not me," she said in reply. "Three is enough. Seven would be wasteful. Don't forget, it's my mother's time and hand-work." One sleeve came free. "Three women in the house times seven coverings would be a lot for her to make." She got the other arm out of the sleeve and folded the cardigan in her lap.

"Too warm? Want the AC?"

She wasn't warm at all—in fact, she might start shivering from the cooling air and fear. "No, I'm just right."

The truck *was* slowing.

"Are we here?"

"Yep. See all those little pines? That's the turnoff. We own a strip of land a mile wide from the highway all the way to the lake."

"Wow. Do you run cattle on it?"

He made the right turn, and Patricia put both hands on the window frame, leaning on her cardigan and stretching her neck out like a dog catching the wind.

But before he could answer—

Bam! The truck slammed into a pothole and Patricia bounced and hit her head on the window frame. But her brains didn't desert her—she whipped the cardigan out into the baby pines, where it hung drunkenly over a branch and bent the little tree over.

"Are you okay?" Chance navigated out of the pothole and looked over, alarmed. "That pothole was not there in the spring when we were here. Sorry."

She made just a bit of a show of putting her hand to her forehead. "I hit my head."

"Only a couple of minutes now. There'll be some salve and Band-Aid patches in the bathroom. Can you hang on?"

"Yes. Thank you," she said meekly, not really pretending now. She'd struck the upper window frame just about dead on the brim of her *Kapp*. It probably had a dent in it. Maybe this was even the same one she'd worn that night in Idaho.

If so, come the next fork in the road and despite what she'd said about Mamm's handwork, the *Kapp* was definitely going out the window.

❦ 20 ❦

GIDEON RODE in the front passenger seat next to Jimmy, who was now fully in the picture about what had happened. He was busy muttering calculations about speed versus distance and how fast they would need to go to close the gap between themselves and Chance's truck. Gideon was pretty sure that arithmetic wasn't going to do the job.

The *gut Gott* would.

That didn't mean they'd sit back and let *der Herr* do all the work, though. Gideon scanned the landscape through the van's big front window, watching for hints of black, a flash of red in the distance—anything that might lead them to Patricia. And all the while in the back of his mind was the insidious, increasing dread that they'd got it all wrong, that Chance and Patricia really had gone to the library or a coffee shop, and they'd hauled Jimmy away from his afternoon nap for nothing. And worse, with every mile they flew down the highway, the thought wouldn't leave him: What if Chance had circled around and gone to Idaho? Or gone east, to Kalispell? Or worst of all, gone north, to Canada?

When he broached this idea to Jimmy, because every possibility had to be considered, Jimmy didn't snort and tell him he was crazy.

"The thought has crossed my mind, too, son," he said reluctantly. "But he'll stay in Montana, I'm pretty sure. That boy has to know that if this girl is in that truck against her will, and he crosses a state line, he'll be committing a federal crime."

"What about Canada? That's a lot closer than Idaho or Wyoming."

"Then that'll be a more serious crime still. But it won't happen. Does Patricia have a passport?"

Gideon was so flummoxed it was a few seconds before he could reply. "Of course not. None of us do. Because of the photograph." Their folk didn't have their pictures taken, even for official documents—it was the equivalent of a graven image. The driving permits the state issued to drive the buggy had no photograph, just a name and address.

Jimmy nodded wisely. "See? They'd never get across the line."

Well, that was one direction he could eliminate. He focused on the southbound direction, and the highway flying away under the tires. Rolling hills, peaks in the distance. Barbed-wire fencing stitching down the edges of ranches. Clumps of pine. A pronghorn startling and leaping away to safety. Ranch country as far as the eye could see, unadorned, rocky, but starkly beautiful to those who lived with and on it.

The speed limit sign read twenty miles per hour slower than they were currently doing, and Jimmy obligingly slowed down five. "State park turnoff," he said by way of explanation.

They passed it—just a narrow road with one lane on each side. Bare, the plants done for the year. Nothing to see.

Except—

"Jimmy, wait. Slow down."

"Why? Every minute we waste, they get farther ahead."

"No, something's out of place. Go back to that turnoff."

Clara had stopped her intent perusal of the land on both sides of the road and leaned forward as Jimmy got the van turned around. When he spun the wheel to make the right turn to the park, she gasped and pointed to the road shoulder.

"Is that a dead crow? Clothes? What is that?"

Jimmy had barely got the van stopped before the two of them leaped out to investigate.

"Our umbrella!" Clara snatched it up and practically shook it in Gideon's face. "It's our umbrella! Remember? Mamm said she took it with her."

"How do you know it's yours and not just some busted thing some litterbug wanted to get rid of?" He didn't dare hope. And yet—he'd seen it—out of place. *Gott* had directed his eyes to that tiny anomaly in the landscape during the split second they'd sped past the turn.

"Here." She turned the handle toward him. *KK.* "Mamm scratched her initials in it so it wouldn't get lost among all the others at church."

Denki, mei Vater. Denki for your blessings. And for this proof that you're leading us right.

"She threw it out the window so we'd know to turn here," he breathed. "Ach, Patricia." They scrambled back into the van with their prize. "Jimmy, they took this road. This is Patricia's umbrella, showing us the way."

Jimmy nodded in admiration. "Smart girl. Come on. Let's hope they don't have far to go. This could get worse than a game of strip poker."

"What's that?" Clara wanted to know, snapping her seatbelt in place.

He flushed. "Never mind, child. Let's get these Chevy horses moving."

❧

CHANCE PULLED UP IN FRONT OF WHAT HE CALLED A *CABIN* and shut off the engine. "Come on. I'll show you where the bathroom is."

As he let her in with a key on his keyring, she took in her new prison. Cabin. Huh. This rustic design, these horrible chandeliers made out of elk antlers, the woven rugs on the polished plank floors ... this was what rich people called a cabin. They ought to see the little *Haus* in Kentucky in which her grandparents had begun their married life. That would be what rich people called a *woodshed*.

He showed her to the bathroom. "I'll see what's in the kitchen. I called the caretakers, but they may not have made it up here with supplies yet."

Caretakers. She shook her head and closed the bathroom door. And locked it.

She used the toilet and washed her hands in a square sink, whose water came out in a little metal trough to make a waterfall. Then she ran a finger under the brim of her *Kapp*. No lump. Maybe she hadn't hit her head that hard, though it had certainly felt like it. But she would still use it for all it was worth if she had to.

She opened the door of the medicine cabinet and there they were, staring back at her right at eye level. Condoms.

She pulled the two boxes out, rearranged the containers of headache pills and hand cream to cover the space, and looked about her. Where would be the last place a young man would look?

She found cleaning supplies in a cabinet close to the door, slid the boxes behind a spray bottle of disinfectant, and tossed a rag over both to make it look like it had been drying there for weeks.

Then she took a deep breath and unlocked the door.

In the kitchen, she found Chance with his head in the refrigerator, considering the contents. "Looks like they didn't get my message. We might have to take a trip to town."

"Let me look." Good grief. "What are you talking about? It's full of food. Maybe not fresh vegetables, but ..." She glanced up at him and closed the door. "I'm starving. Why don't I make supper?"

His face lit up as though he'd thought she would be angry with him. Angrier. "Yeah? That'd be great. We can always go to town tomorrow."

"How far is it?"

"Libby."

Oh. Oh, no. She was not going to Libby under any circumstances. Shaking her head, she said, "There's plenty for breakfast, too. Let's not worry about it."

"So ... you'll stay for the weekend?"

To her immense relief, he went over to the sliding glass door to take in what she had to admit was a stupendous view of the lake, ringed with cliffs rising straight out of the water. They were up pretty high, on a bluff overlooking the pristine wilderness around the park.

"It's not like I can drive your truck out of here, Chance. You brought me here against my will, so I don't have a choice but to stay."

"Aw, Patty, don't be like that."

"I *am* like that," she said firmly, maybe a little too firmly, but only because she couldn't allow her voice to tremble. "You are going to take me home in the morning. In the meantime, I will make supper and then I will go to bed. In a room of my own. Alone."

His chest rose and fell in a big sigh. "Can we at least do something after supper? It's only five o'clock."

"Like what?"

"I don't know. Watch TV. Play a game."

"I like chess. Or checkers. No Monopoly, though. That always makes me cranky."

He stared at her. "I was thinking more along the lines of *Call of Duty*. But we could do *Elder Scrolls* if you like that better."

She had no idea what either of those were. "Let me figure out supper first, all right? Why don't you set the table?"

"We usually just eat in front of the TV."

She could see the big, squashy leather sofa from here, with the TV mounted over the fireplace like people used to mount trophy animal heads. What happened if someone spilled their food on that expensive leather? *Never mind. Not your problem.*

"If I'm making supper, we eat it at the table. If you have things to do, I'll find the plates and silverware myself."

At this, he turned from the window and headed for the granite-topped counter, under whose glossy earth-toned length were rows of cabinets and drawers. "I got it."

From the fridge she pulled eggs and cheese, the latter only a week past its best-by date. In the pantry, which lay behind a big door designed to look like a twin to the fridge, she found cans of green chile, an unopened bag of flour, and a dozen bottles of spices, all unopened. She chose one of red chile powder and one of dried oregano.

It wouldn't be exactly like Susanna Miller's yummy break-fast bake—there was no shortening to be seen anywhere so she couldn't make dumplings—but it would come close. There was no milk to make the white sauce, either, but water would do in a pinch.

The eggs had been in the fridge a while, she noticed when she cracked them, but they were usable. She shredded cheese, layered it with green chile, added eggs to the white sauce, and sprinkled in a teaspoon of each of the spices. Then the whole thing went into the oven, which, thank goodness, was propane. At least she knew what she was doing with that.

No dumplings, no cornmeal muffins, no vegetables.

No family. No help.

But she wouldn't starve.

When she carried the steaming casserole over to the table forty minutes later, its surface bubbly and golden and smelling delicious, her stomach growled. And when Chance tasted it, he groaned with pleasure. "This is so good. I don't know how you did it."

She lifted her head from her silent grace—and a plea to *Gott in Himmel* to help her find a way out of this beautiful cage. "I can teach you next time." She took a bite and savored it. It was *gut. Denki, Susanna.* "Because it looks like we'll be having the same thing for breakfast."

"Suits me."

It was an eight by ten casserole dish and they ate the whole thing. Patricia cleared the table while Chance wandered off into the living room.

"Aren't you going to help me with the dishes?" She held out a dish towel.

"No...?" He sounded like she'd asked him to take a leap off the cliff. "The dishwasher is right there."

"Then you don't get any breakfast, and I don't use a dish-washer." She turned to the sink, found the dish soap, and ran hot water. "I may be your prisoner, but I'm not your servant."

He was at her side in a moment, reaching for the dish towel. "You're not a prisoner. I would never do that to you, Patty. This is supposed to be fun." He paused, and picked up the dripping plate she'd set on another towel. There was no drain rack. "I mean, I'm having fun. A beautiful woman just made me supper like magic, out of nothing. We're alone in my favorite place in the world. What could be better?"

She rolled her eyes toward him in an *are you kidding?* expression. "A woman who actually wants to be here?"

His face fell, and he dried the rest of the dishes in silence while she scrubbed cooked cheese off the casserole dish.

"You're mean," he said at last. "Just like all the rest of them."

"I am *not* mean." She handed him the dish. "I'm like any other girl in the world who likes to be asked what she wants, and to be taken seriously when she answers."

"I take you seriously. You're the most serious thing in my life."

This was not the time to remind him she was not in his life at all. She'd been a fool to let him believe he was, during her brief *Rumspringe*. That had been her mistake.

"You didn't when I asked you to take me to the Wengerds'. Or when I asked you to stop in Mountain Home so I could walk back. You ignored me and took me forty miles away from my family and—" Oh, dear, here came the tears. She wailed, "And nobody knows where I am." She let herself go, pulling the dishtowel out of his hands and sobbing all her grief and fear into it.

"Aw, Patty, don't cry. Come here." Clumsy, uncertain, he attempted to take her into his arms.

But there was only one man on this earth in whose arms she wanted to be.

She spun away, dropped the dish towel, and ran blindly across the living room for the door.

"Patty—! Whoa—!"

She whirled just in time to see his boot land on the dish-towel on the glossy floor. He skated one-legged for a foot, arms flailing, and went over backward. He landed with a crash that rattled the walls just as the door burst open and Gideon Miller barreled through it like he was loaded for bear.

※ 21 ※

THE CIRCLE M RANCH

Sunday, August 21

THE PREACHER'S sermon the next morning came from Luke 18 and 19.

> *There was in a city a judge, which feared not God, neither regarded man: And there was a widow in that city; and she came unto him, saying, Avenge me of mine adversary...*

Appropriate that they should hear about judgment this morning, Gideon thought from his place among the *Gmay* in the big living room at the Circle M, doing his best not to glance to the left, where Patricia's bowed head was just visible on the far side of Clara. While the *gut Gott* may have directed them to the Madison hunting cabin to work out His plan to save Patricia, it was up to worldly hands now to work out Chance's judgment.

Jimmy had been all for calling the sheriff, right there at the cabin. He'd become quite agitated about it, too, especially when it had taken a few minutes for Chance to recover from the whack his head had received on that hard floor.

Also the Lord's judgment, as far as Gideon was concerned.

But once they were all back at the King home and a sobbing Kate was willing to let go of Patricia, Jimmy had convinced him and Arlon to go with him over to the Rocking Diamond to tell the Madisons what their son had done. Jimmy had managed to get his licks in despite Gideon's calm recital of the facts and Arlon's solemn observation that as his parents, they were morally required to make the punishment fit the crime.

"That boy kidnapped that innocent Amish girl really believing that he was going to marry her—and not in a strictly legal sense, either," Jimmy had burst out, unable to keep quiet. "I don't know what kind of delusional misfit you folks have brought up, but I am seconds away from calling in the sheriff to deal with him."

Gideon had never thought he'd see the day when Arlon King and Brock Madison agreed on anything, but they'd agreed that each would handle their own offspring and there would be no need to bring in the law. Then there was a bunch of nonsense from the Madison side about there being no real harm done, and a huge effort on the King side at godly forgiveness and self-control, and they had taken their leave.

"I don't like it," Jimmy had grumbled. "But if you folks change your minds, I'm first in line to be a witness for the prosecution." Then he'd taken his pay and their heartfelt thanks for his part in Patricia's rescue, and was still grumbling when the van rumbled away down the King lane.

But that had been yesterday, and was now in the past.

Gideon was thankful that, here in the present, he and

Patricia were once again in the same room together, safe in *Gottes* hand.

When the final hymn was sung and people had made their way out on the broad decks to wait while the room was turned over for the fellowship meal, Gideon wasted no time in finding Patricia. Clara discreetly turned to someone on her other side, leaving Gideon looking down into Patricia's tired eyes.

"You didn't sleep?" he asked softly. "I wondered if you'd be able to."

"A little," she admitted. "But every time I dozed off, I was back in that truck, leaning out the window while we drove past you at the feed store."

"Me? That was Tobias."

"Not in my dream," she said, shaking her head. With a sigh, she went on, "Gideon, I was never so frightened in my life. I'm honestly wondering if I can ever walk on that highway again without fainting from fear every time a pickup passes me."

"You won't have to walk to the Rocking Diamond, at least," he said. "Your *dat* told them you weren't coming back."

"And this time both of us mean it." She tried to smile.

"Is Clara still going to drive you to the quilt shop for work? Or are you going to ride your bicycle?"

Before Patricia could reply, Clara said over her shoulder, "*Ja*, I am. After this, I'm never complaining about it again."

"Then I'll pick her up after work," Gideon said. Clara gave a brief nod and that was that.

"*Denki,*" Patricia said. "I'm grateful. But are you sure? Ranch work doesn't keep a clock."

"I've already cleared it with Reuben. My cousins will pitch in if something goes wrong." He dared to touch her wrist, right there in public. "They're just as shocked and concerned as I am."

Luckily, anyone watching was distracted by Naomi's coming to the door and announcing lunch was ready. While he wanted to sit with Patricia, there would be time enough for that. She needed her family, especially with her ordeal following so closely on the loss of Aendi Annie. Fellowship and food and family ... in his experience, those three went a long way toward helping a person heal.

After lunch, folks with young families headed home, and the older ones followed suit around three o'clock. With the crowd thinned, he found Patricia with his cousin Malena and Alden Stolzfus, leaning on the deck rail and watching Clara and Calvin Yoder amble down the river path together.

"I hope she knows that two times out of three, he falls in," Malena said with an air of long experience.

"I'm sure she does," Patricia replied. "I'm also pretty sure he can haul himself out."

"Are they courting?" Alden asked, trying not to smile and failing.

"She hasn't told me so, but it's pretty hard not to think so when they walk out like that, right in front of everyone."

Alden just shook his head while Malena slipped an arm around Patricia's waist and gave her a squeeze. "How's the wedding quilt coming?"

"Do you have to call it that?" Patricia complained, but she was smiling.

"I heard about the family tradition." His cousin slid Gideon a mischievous look. "What do you think, Gideon? Do you believe it?"

"I do." He'd be in for so much teasing, but right now, like Calvin, he didn't care. "And even if I didn't, I still want to make it come true."

Alden whooped and Malena let out a peal of laughter that

made Aendi Naomi turn from her conversation and raise her eyebrows. "That's the spirit," Alden said.

On a wave of defiant happiness, he said to Patricia, "Have you ever been up to Grossmammi's orchard?"

"Only once, but it was winter and there wasn't much to see but snow and bare trees."

"It's better now. *Kumm mit.*" And with a grin at Malena, who was looking as though she couldn't wait to tell all her siblings, he ushered Patricia along the deck to the gate that gave onto the path up the hillside.

"You are a brave and foolish man," Patricia told him, half laughing. "But luckily, Calvin is making such a scene with Clara today that no one will notice us."

"The foolish part of me doesn't care if they do," he told her, taking her hand to help her up the slope. "So does the brave part, come to think of it."

He didn't let go of her hand.

She didn't let go of his, either.

They walked into the box canyon's mouth to see the trees heavy with fruit. "Look at this one," he said, touching a cluster on the nearest tree with his free hand. "These are red now. I was up here only a little while ago, and they were still mostly green."

"They know they don't have much time," Patricia said softly. "Aendi Annie told me once that it can snow as early as Labor Day. That's not far away."

"Right after my brother's wedding."

"Goodness me, you're right. What a day that will be! Are you going to be his *Neuwesitzer?*"

"He asked me. And Seth, too, of course."

"And Sylvia? Who did she choose?"

"Her cousins, Bethany and Sharon. They're staying for the wedding and roundup, then heading home."

"I'm glad I don't have to go anywhere," she said softly. "I'm glad our home is right here in the Siksika. I never want to leave it."

"I'm glad to hear that, because I don't, either." He smiled into her eyes, but said no more. They hadn't even had a proper date yet, though his heart had made its choice and there was no shadow of turning.

In the shade of the old apple tree, their hands entwined, she leaned against him, the two of them breathing in the sweet scent of apples.

It was time to speak, he decided. To make a start. "Can I give you a ride home from singing tonight?"

"Aren't you going to ask my sister to ask me?" she teased.

"I think she's busy. I'm taking the direct route."

"Me too." She smiled up at him as though her answer were a given. "*Ja*, of course you can."

"And on Thursday when I pick you up from work, how about we go for ice cream?"

"I'd never say *neh* to ice cream."

"And at Tobias's wedding, can I ask Sylvia to partner us for supper?"

"If I don't ask her first."

Happiness swelled under his breastbone and caught in his throat. "Listen to us. At this rate, I'll be making an appointment to kiss you."

"Sadly, all my appointments are closed. You'll just have to take pot luck, Gideon Miller."

"With you, I'd never want to just take," he said, his teasing smile fading to certainty. He turned to her and took her other hand in his. "I'd want to give. And accept. And never, ever take you for granted."

"I'd like that," she whispered. "And the same for me. But for right now, will you please kiss me?"

He leaned his forehead on hers. "I'd never say *neh* to that," he echoed.

His lips found hers, and he thought he might melt from the softness, the sweetness of hers. His heart pounded as he gathered her into his arms. Was it possible to lift right off the ground from sheer happiness?

Denki, Aendi Annie. He sent his last coherent thought heavenward. *Denki for the tradition of the wedding quilt.*

SETH MILLER COULDN'T KEEP his feet still, or contain his impatience to be outside. To be moving. He'd seen Clara King walking out with Calvin Yoder. He'd seen Gideon taking the path to the orchard, where no doubt he and Patricia would come back engaged or at least officially courting. In the east district, where it was off Sunday, Susanna and Stephen were spending the afternoon with Mamm and Luke, and Tobias and Sylvia, gathered around the table talking over the latter's wedding plans for next week.

Everyone in his family had inexplicably found someone to love. Well, not inexplicably. Seth knew as well as anyone that *Gottes* hand had been very busy in the Miller family over the last year or two.

But the question still nagged him. *Why not me? When will it be my turn?*

There was no shortage of young women in the Siksika Valley. But he hadn't felt that nudge, that urge to be close to someone, that his brothers had clearly felt. And it must have been quite a nudge for Gideon and Patricia to suddenly see each other in a different light. Not simply because of Chance Madison running off with her. Something had been going on with his brother before that. But what an unlikely pair—two people who barely had a civil word for one another, and now they were up in the orchard canoodling.

At least, if it were him and a girl he was sweet on, he'd be attempting to canoodle.

He had intended to walk toward the ridge to see the progress on Adam's house. He hadn't been up here in a week or two, and from what Adam said, the house was nearly ready for Kate and their wedding day.

But he'd been so deep in thought he'd walked right past the house in its meadow of wildflowers and found himself up on the ridge proper. Good thing he'd come to himself, or he'd have wound up on the Rocking Diamond.

He blinked. Speaking of, who was coming from that direction?

In a moment he recognized her. Zefra Harris. Was she going for a hike? She couldn't be coming over on some business. Not even Brock Madison would disturb his Amish neighbors on a church Sunday.

She wasn't even out of breath when she joined him on the rocky ridge. "Hey, Seth. I'm glad I ran into you. Mrs Madison sent me over, but I've been trying to figure out how to do this without disturbing the family. I know you have church today."

"She sent you over? To do what? Isn't it your day off?"

She nodded. "Me and Matty are going swimming under the bridge as soon as I get back. But she wanted me to deliver this."

She handed him a letter, folded in thirds but not sealed or in an envelope. He could see neat typing through the paper.

"Who's it for?" he asked, puzzled.

"Patricia, but really for the whole family. It's from Chance."

He resisted the temptation to ball it up and throw it away. "I don't think Patricia wants to hear from him. I know her family doesn't."

"I wouldn't, either, after what he pulled." She shrugged. "Well, use your discretion. Read it if you want. Give it to her dad, maybe, and let him decide. My work here is done, and my kid is waiting for me."

With a smile, she turned, made her way back down the path, and was soon out of sight in the pines.

Feeling a little bemused, he couldn't resist opening the piece of paper he'd just been given permission to read.

Dear Patty and family,

I wanted to let you know how sorry I am about what happened on Saturday. I was stupid and misread the situation. I've learned some lessons about listening and that no means no. I still think you're the most wonderful girl I know, but this is the last time I'll burden you with saying it.

I'm leaving tomorrow for military college in Alabama. Dad knows a guy on the board and they said they'd be happy to accept me. I'll take my time driving down there, maybe visit a national park or two and get my head together. Class starts in September.

I'm sorry I won't get to learn how to make an egg and chile casse-role. I wish you the very best in the future.

Yours truly,
Chance Madison

"Good grief," Seth muttered. He still wanted to ball up the letter and throw it away, but that wasn't his place. It would be up to Arlon King.

Still, one thing had caught his interest. National parks. This was the third time he'd heard about people visiting the national parks—and the second time had been from his cousin Daniel's wife, Lovina. That was how they'd met again. She was on a tour of some of the national parks with a bunch of Amish folks from Whinburg Township, and the van had broken down in the Siksika. She'd wound up here at the Circle M completely by chance, and there was Daniel, who'd never gotten over her after a summer long ago.

The third time was something Susanna had said the other day. She corresponded with their cousin Emily Kuepfer on Prince Edward Island, and apparently someone she knew was organizing a trip like the one Lovina had been on. There would be a married couple acting as chaperone, of course, but the rest would be a bunch of *Youngie* from all over.

Three times. If that wasn't a heavy hint from *der Herr*, he didn't know what was.

Suddenly Seth's restless feet had a good reason to move. After roundup, he'd have his pay. He'd be able to afford a train ticket to join the trip. He'd never seen any of the national parks except Glacier, which was hard to miss since it was practically in their backyard. Maybe now was the time to broaden his horizons.

He jogged across the meadow. He'd hand this stupid letter to Arlon and go track down his brother. If he promised to have Gideon's buggy back before singing, he could drive over to the Inn right now and ask Susanna what she knew about Emily's travel plans.

Surely a trip like that would satisfy not only the restlessness that had plagued him lately, but the loneliness, too, watching all his siblings so happy with the people *Gott* had led them to.

Then maybe he, too, could get serious about the business of courtship.

THE END

AFTERWORD

NOTE FROM ADINA

I hope you've enjoyed the tenth book about the Miller family on the Circle M Ranch and at the Wild Rose Amish Inn. If you subscribe to my newsletter, you'll hear about new releases in the series, my research in Montana, and snippets about quilting and writing and chickens—my favorite subjects!

I hope you'll join me by subscribing at
www.subscribepage.com/shelley-adina

Haven't read the first book in the Amish Cowboys of Montana series? You'll find *The Amish Cowboy* on my store, www.moonshellbooks.com. And while you're there, be sure to browse my other Amish novels set in beautiful Whinburg Township, Pennsylvania, beginning with *The Wounded Heart*.

Following is a glossary of the Pennsylvania Dutch words used in this book. But first, here's a sneak peek at *The Amish Cowboy's Journey*, Seth Miller's story!

THE AMISH COWBOY'S JOURNEY © ADINA SENFT

It isn't the road ahead that wears you out, it's the burr in your sock.
  —Mountain Home Amish proverb

Unlike his siblings, who have put down roots in the Amish community in the Siksika Valley, Seth Miller is the restless one—always looking to the horizon and wondering what lies beyond it. When a group of Amish *Youngie* plan a van trip to visit several national parks, Seth decides to join them. It's only for a few weeks, and it might satisfy that urge and help him settle down.

Shy Beth Stolzfus, who seems to be invisible most of the time, surprises everyone by announcing she wants to go, too. She's tired of being overlooked and underappreciated—maybe this trip will give her a chance to stretch her wings and be someone different. Someone who might catch the eye of one of the other Amish adventurers. Not Seth Miller, that's for sure. He's already made it clear in a hundred ways that he's not interested.

Except that travel can bring out the best in someone as well as the worst. Beth proves to have a level head when one of the other travelers needs help. And her eyes seem to speak a language all their own. Surrounded by the beauty of God's handiwork in nature, Seth slowly comes to realize that what his heart has been longing for may not be over the horizon after all. It may be much closer to home.

The Montana Millers. They believe in faith, family, and the land. They'll need all three when love comes to Mountain Home!

GLOSSARY

Spelling and definitions from Eugene S. Stine, *Pennsylvania German Dictionary* (Birdboro, PA: Pennsylvania German Society, 1996).

Words used:

Ach, neh! Oh no!

Aendi: auntie

Bischt du okay? Are you okay?

Bidde: please

Bob: bun (hair)

Bruder: brother

Daadi Haus: grandfather house

Dat: Dad

Deitsch: Pennsylvania Dutch

Denki, denkes: thank you, thanks

Dochder(e): daughter, daughters

Druwwel: trouble

Dummkopf: stupid

Englisch: not-Amish people, English language

Englischer: English person

Enschuldichung: excuse me

Herr, der: the Lord

Fraa: wife

Gedunner: racket, noise

Genug: enough

Gmay: congregation, church body

Gott: God

Gott in Himmel: God in heaven

Gottes wille: God's will

Grossmammi: great-grandmother

Guder mariye: Good morning, good day

Guder nacht: Good night

Guder owed: Good afternoon/evening

Gut: good

Haus: house

Ischt gut, denki: It's good, thanks

Ja: yes

Kaffee: coffee

Kapp: women's prayer covering

Kind, kleiner Kind, Kinner: child, small child, children

Kumm mit: come along (lit. come with)

Kummst du jetzt: Come now

Lieber Gott in Himmel: dear God in Heaven

Liewi: dear

Maedsche(r): girl, girls

Mamm: Mom

Mann, dei: your man, husband

Maud: maid

Middagessen: midday meal

Narre: idiots

Neh: no

Neuwesitzer: lit. side-sitter, or supporter

Nix? From *nichts*, Is it not?

Onkel: uncle

Ordnung: The order, rule, or discipline adhered to by each congregation

Roascht: traditional wedding dish of chicken and stuffing

Rumspringe: The time of running around for Amish youth

Schulhaus: schoolhouse

Schweschder, mei: my sister

Sohn: son

Verhuddelt: confused, mixed up

Wunderbaar: wonderful

Youngie: young people

The Highest Mountain

The Sweetest Song

The Heart's Return (novella)

৯&

Breaking Faith

Grounds to Believe

Pocketful of Pearls

Sounds in the Night

Over Her Head

৯&

Glory Prep (faith-based young adult)

Glory Prep

The Fruit of My Lipstick

Be Strong and Curvaceous

Who Made You a Princess?

Tidings of Great Boys

The Chic Shall Inherit the Earth

ABOUT THE AUTHOR

USA Today bestselling author Adina Senft grew up in a plain house church, where she was often asked by outsiders if she was Amish (the answer was no). She holds a PhD in Creative Writing from Lancaster University in the UK. Adina was the winner of RWA's RITA Award for Best Inspirational Novel in 2005 for *Grounds to Believe*, a finalist for that award in 2006 for *Pocketful of Pearls*, and was a Christy Award finalist in 2009 for *The Fruit of My Lipstick*. She appeared in the 2016 documentary film *Love Between the Covers*, is a popular speaker and convention panelist, and has been a guest on many podcasts, including Worldshapers and Realm of Books.

She writes steampunk adventure and mystery as Shelley Adina; and as Charlotte Henry, writes classic Regency romance. When she's not writing, Adina is usually quilting, sewing historical costumes, or enjoying the garden with her flock of rescued chickens.

facebook.com/adinasenft

pinterest.com/shelleyadina

bookbub.com/authors/adina-senft

instagram.com/shelleyadinasenft

bsky.app/profile/shelleyadinasenft.bsky.social